To Josh Omang, for his amazing help and dedication on the cover for my book. Couldn't have asked for a better friend and illustrator. Thank you so much for everything.

To Shannon Streather, for her help and commitment in proof reading and feedback on my work to help me push myself further and expand my thinking.

Shay Blair

BLOODLUST

AUSTIN MACAULEY PUBLISHERS™
LONDON • CAMBRIDGE • NEW YORK • SHARJAH

Copyright © Shay Blair 2023

The right of Shay Blair to be identified as author of this work has been asserted by the author in accordance with sections 77 and 78 of the Copyright, Designs and Patents Act 1988.

All rights reserved. No part of this publication may be reproduced, stored in a retrieval system, or transmitted in any form or by any means, electronic, mechanical, photocopying, recording, or otherwise, without the prior permission of the publishers.

Any person who commits any unauthorised act in relation to this publication may be liable to criminal prosecution and civil claims for damages.

This is a work of fiction. Names, characters, businesses, places, events, locales, and incidents are either the products of the author's imagination or used in a fictitious manner. Any resemblance to actual persons, living or dead, or actual events is purely coincidental.

A CIP catalogue record for this title is available from the British Library.

ISBN 9781398494626 (Paperback)
ISBN 9781398494633 (ePub e-book)

www.austinmacauley.com

First Published 2023
Austin Macauley Publishers Ltd®
1 Canada Square
Canary Wharf
London
E14 5AA

To Austin Macauley Publishers, without whom this book would not be possible. To the staff at Focus Charity, who believed in me. And to my family, for all their support and love during my journey.

Table of Contents

Chapter 1: The Start of a New Era	9
Chapter 2: New Beginnings	22
Chapter 3: Secrets Out	32
Chapter 4: Broken Hearts	44
Chapter 5: The Truth	54
Chapter 6: Engagement Party	66
Chapter 7: Hunters	76
Chapter 8: New Wolf	92
Chapter 9: The Invitation	104
Chapter 10: You Give Werewolves a Bad Name	115
Chapter 11: The Dream	124
Chapter 12: Fight with the Hunters	136
Chapter 13 The Ball	141
Chapter 14: New Vampire	153
Chapter 15: Missing	160
Chapter 16: The Island of Wonder	167

Chapter 17: The Legend	**176**
Chapter 18: Spirit of Keres	**184**
Chapter 19: Celebrate	**194**

Chapter 1
The Start of a New Era

It all started when my older brother and I moved to a small town in London, called Greenwich. It was a mysterious town, full of life and light. My name is Samuel, Sam for short, and this is how my secret became the one thing that destroyed me and everyone I love.

2017

Evie wakes up to the sunlight that streams through her open window, she can hear the birds chirping. Evie rolls over, looks at her alarm clock and sighs, one whole hour until school starts. She reluctantly gets up, heads into her closet to get dressed and then goes downstairs.

"Good morning!" Her mum says. Evie looks at her with sleep deprived eyes as she yawns. Evie has long brown hair that is tied in a pony. She is wearing denim trouser with a white vest top. Her mum has short black hair and is wearing her nurse uniform.

"Morning," Evie replies, picking up the cereal box and pouring it into a bowl, before moving to the fridge to get the milk.

"Where is Adam?" Evie asks looking around the kitchen for her over-the-top annoying younger brother.

"Adam has already headed to school with your dad. I must get to work, so you'll have to make your own way to school. We won't be back until late; I've left money on the counter for you to get something to eat later. Have a good day!" Her mum tells her before leaving. Evie eats her cereal before heading outside to wait for the school bus, when it arrives, she gets on and looks around before realising she doesn't know anyone. She sulks down the aisle and into a seat, where she puts on her headphones, for the rest of the journey.

When she arrives, her best friend, Brooke comes running towards her squealing, and hugs her. Evie and Brooke have known each other since they were five and met in preschool, she loves her best friend but sometimes feels like she can be competitive. Brooke has long, curly black hair with brown eyes. She wears glasses and is tall.

"Evie!" She says excitedly.

"Brooke, how was your summer?" Evie asks.

"It was amazing. We went to this great lake house in Arizona, it had a hot tub," Brooke tells her.

"Sounds like you had fun," Evie replies.

"I did what about you? What did you do this summer?" Brooke asks.

"Same as always. Revised a lot," Evie answers.

"Boring! You need a life, take a risk. Have an adventure, we only live once," Brooke says. They walk towards the school; it is three-stories high with glass windows. Once inside, they look around at the familiar scene, on the right of the door there are stairs with kids sitting around and chatting.

The rest of the hall has lockers spread out and a vending machine at the end, in between the bathrooms.

"I've missed this bubbly atmosphere," Evie says.

"It just got a whole lot less bubbly," Brooke tells her looking down the hall where Mia and Mandy are handing out flyers. Mandy is tall, with dark skin and long red hair. Mia has blonde hair and green eyes; her skin is pale. They both groan in unison as the ice queens notices them.

"Oh look, here comes the loser squad," Mandy says to Mia. Mia offers them a flyer. The flyer is green and white and has been printed out on a computer.

"I'll pass," Brooke tells her.

"Good, we didn't want you anyway," Mandy replies flipping her hair and smirking at Mia. "It's just school policy to offer everyone a chance on the cheerleading team."

"School policy? Since when?" Evie asks.

"Since this year," Mandy snaps.

"Ignore her Evie. She's just sour. Hey, isn't it true that your cheer squad placed last at regionals last year?" Brooke asks her.

"That was just a mistake. We should have come first. The judges were biased," Mia tells her trying to impress Mandy.

"Well, cheerleading is meant to be all about spirit. You guys say you're a family, but half the team feared you. Once the mayor found out about that she just couldn't place you first," Brooke says.

"Do you think I'm stupid? I know it was you who told your mum about the bullying," Mandy says.

"There is no proof. Just because my mum is the mayor doesn't mean anything. For all you know, Mia could have told her," Brooke points out.

"Mia wouldn't do that. She's loyal," Mandy replies.

"Yeah, we thought that too," Brooke responds looking Mia up and down with disgust before glaring back at Mandy. "Anyway, maybe we will try-out. Evie was just saying how she wanted to do something new this year," Brooke responds.

"I was?" Evie asks confused. Brooke elbows her in the side as if to say play along. "I mean, I was," Evie nods her head as conformation as Brooke face palms with a sigh dejectedly, she can see Mandy smirking and Mia trying to cover up the fact that she's laughing with the stupid flyers.

"Great we will see you at try-outs," Mia says cheerily. Brooke snatches the flyer out Mia's hand before grabbing Evie and storming away, muttering under her breath about Mandy.

Further down the corridor, Sam walks past them looking around lost. He sees two lads standing at a locker talking in hushed voices like they're scheming something.

"Hey, I'm new here, and I'm supposed to attend a welcome assembly. Could you point me to the sport department?" He asks them as he slowly approaches, unsure of how they'd react.

"Sure. We were just heading there." The taller one of replies closing his locker, he gestures for Sam to follow.

"I'm Jake, by the way," he says extending his hand.

"Sam," he replies shaking it with a smile on his face.

"Well, Sam, it's nice to meet you. This is Taylor," Jake tells him pointing at his friend. Jake is tall, with brown eyes and light hair; he has a nice build you could tell he works out. Taylor is shorter with dark hair; he isn't as built as his Jake. Sam is of average height with light dirty blonde hair, he walks with a swag.

"This town is fairly boring. What made you move here?" Taylor asks trying to engage in conversation.

"I fancied a change," Sam replies as they all head into the hall. The hall is big, on one side there are bleachers full of students and on the other is a stage where the teachers are sitting chatting among themselves. A young girl stands among them. Sam follows Jake and Taylor up the stairs to find a seat. Once everyone is settled the principal stands and goes to the podium at the front of the stage and starts to welcome everyone back to another year. After he's finished, he steps back, and the young girl takes the stage.

"Lets' give you the rundown," Jake says to Sam.

"Rundown? What on?" Sam asks confused.

"How things work around here," Taylor replies. Sam looks at them like they're talking nonsense.

"Taylor and I are jocks. That is Mandy," he says pointing at the girl on stage. "She is head cheerleader with her best friend Mia. Those two girls there are Brooke and Evie, things are a little sour between them and Mia, because we all grew up together, but when Mandy moved here from New York three years ago, Mia ditched them for her. Brooke never got over it, she acts like it was the biggest crime of the century. Evie doesn't care as much, because she just wants a trouble-free life. I think that's everything," Jake says.

"You forgot something," Taylor tells him.

"What?" Jake asks looking at him confused. Taylor clears his throat.

"Mandy is a two-faced bitch who nobody likes. We all just pretend to, because we must. She bullies people. If you want my advice, stay away. Getting involved with her is trouble. Oh, and Jake is dating Mia," Taylor points out.

"Okay, that's good to know. Thank you," Sam says, slightly unsure of what just happened.

"Anytime," Taylor replies, Jake looks at him.

"What?" Taylor asks. Jake just shakes his head. Mandy finishes her speech, and everyone starts heading out the hall.

"Jake!" Mia shouts running towards him. Jake embraces her, as Mandy saunters over.

"Something wicked comes this way," Taylor says before walking off he looks at Sam to follow.

Later that day Evie walks round the corner and collides with Sam. Her books fall onto the floor, scattering about.

"Careful," Sam says bending down to help her pick them up.

"Sorry, I didn't see you there," Evie replies looking up into his eyes. He smiles and they stand up, he passes her the books.

"It's cool. No damage done," Sam tells her, Evie smiles at him.

"I'm Evie," she says offering her hand.

"I know," Sam tells her. Evie looks at him, concerned, and he realises what he said, "I mean I know who you are because Jake told me earlier. I'm Sam." He shakes her hand.

"Well Sam it's nice to meet you," Evie responds.

"You too," Sam replies. They stand there looking at each other for a few minutes, still holding hands. Evie notices and clears her throat.

"I should get going. Have to get to cheer practise," she says.

"You're a cheerleader?" Sam asks with an eyebrow raised.

"Yeah, is it a surprise?" She asks him.

"A little, you don't strike me as a cheerleader type. More of a bookworm," he answers.

"That's because I am. The only reason I'm doing this, is because my friend wants to prove a point," Evie tells him.

"What's the point?" Sam asks.

"That Mandy can't control everything," Evie replies. Sam looks at her.

"Well then, good luck. You'll make a great cheerleader," he says. Evie walks off smiling and Sam watches her go.

At cheer practise, Evie and Brooke get up to audition. Brooke is buzzing to go, while Evie is unsure.

"It's a pretty basic routine. The floor is yours, good luck." Mia says reassuringly. Brooke and Evie start dancing, the routine that lasts five minutes. When they've finished, they sit down panting.

"Congratulations girls. That routine was impossible to mess up and yet you managed it anyway," Mandy says smirking.

"Mandy!" Mia exclaims angrily. Mandy rolls her eyes and ignores her.

"I'll post the list tomorrow to tell you who made it." Her eyes fall on Evie and Brooke, "And who didn't," she tells everyone. Everyone gets up and leaves, talking about getting a spot. Brooke pushes past Mia, and Evie follows, wishing she never showed up.

"She is just cruel," Taylor tells Jake as they are sitting on the bleachers watching.

"You don't have to be so mean," Mia says to Mandy.

"God what is up with you today?" Mandy asks, not even looking at her, but instead picking up the clipboard with the sheet of names on.

"Nothing, it's just you criticise everything and they weren't even bad," Mia replies frustrated.

"Oh please. It was painful to watch. Besides, you were the one who spent the past two years saying that they weren't good enough to join," Mandy reminds her.

"Yes, well the difference is, I actually feel bad about that and I am trying to make up for it," Mia points out.

"Why? You chose me, remember? You had the choice three years ago, about who you wanted to be friends with, and you chose me, the cool popular girl from New York over the two losers from here," Mandy says.

"Maybe that was a mistake, and they're not losers, so stop calling them it," Mia replies.

"You don't mean that, I am the best thing to ever happen to you," Mandy tells her.

"Are you?" Mia asks daringly. Mandy looks taken back.

"Yes, I know you. You love having power. That's something you'll never give up," she replies.

"You're right. I do love having power, and being joint captains of this team means that I can decide who does and doesn't get on the team and I'm saying I want Brooke and Evie," Mia says sternly, Mandy sighs disappointedly and throws the clipboard onto the table.

"Lets' make a deal, because I know you've had a bad summer, I'll let you sleep on it and if tomorrow morning you haven't changed your mind, then we will let one of them join the team. But I get to pick which one," Mandy responds.

"Why do you get to pick?" Mia asks, crossing her arms.

"Because I'm better than you and because I don't care what you think, and nobody cares what you have to say," Mandy tells her turning around.

"That's where you're wrong. People do care what I think, especially the mayor. She was more than happy to hear what I had to say about the way you run the cheerleading team and how you treat people," Mia points out. Mandy stops before looking Mia in the eye, anger burning.

"It was you! You were the one to tell the mayor last year, so we lost," she says angrily.

"Yes," Mia says shrugging it off without a care.

"Why? Why would you do that?" Mandy asks stomping her foot.

"Because I'm tired of your constant and pointless drama. I'm tired of the way you treat people and I'm tired of you," Mia replies stepping towards her. Mandy stares her dead in the eye, before stepping closer, the anger taking over.

"I hate you!" She yells swinging for her, she slaps Mia across the face. Mia screams and tackles Mandy to the floor as they fight.

"Ooh girl fight," Taylor says. Jake looks at him before running over and pulling Mia off, he drags her out the hall kicking and screaming. Taylor gets up and follows, leaving Mandy all alone.

Sam arrives home and finds his brother Alex in the sitting room, drinking blood. He casually looks up when he hears his brother arriving. Alex has dark hair and is tall.

"Good your back, I want to hear all about your first day. But first I got you a gift," Alex says as a woman comes out of the next room and walks towards him. Sam smiles at his brother before sinking his teeth into the woman's neck. Alex goes back over to the man on the sofa, later when they finish, Alex and Sam take a walk through the woods.

"So how was it? Nobody found out about you, did they?" Alex asks suspiciously.

"No, don't worry I kept our secret. And as for my day, it was really good," Sam replies, Alex looks at him.

"Ah, you met someone. Who is she?" He asks.

"Her name is Evie, and how did you know?" Sam asks.

"Please, I know when my baby brother has met someone. You get this certain twinkle in your eyes," Alex tells him.

"Okay, so do you," Sam says.

"I know, we both do," Alex replies.

"The only thing is, you haven't had it since Vikki," Sam tells him. Alex stops smiling.

"I miss her and it's killing me not knowing what happened to her. Is she dead or is she alive? And what about Lizzie, what has happened to her?" Alex says. Sam looks at him, and they sit on a log.

"I know, I miss Lizzie too," Sam tells him. Alex looks at him.

"Do you ever think about that day? And how we lost both of them, because we were too selfish to let go?" Alex asks.

"Yes! All the time," Sam answers.

Flashback to 1856

"Alex!" Sam shouts holding a young girl in his arms. Alex runs over with another girl.

"Lizzie!" He says bending down next to her.

"What happened?" The girl asks.

"She didn't get away from the explosion quick enough," Sam replies. Alex looks at her.

"Vikki, please you have to help her," Alex begs.

"No, leave me," Lizzie says. Vikki had long, ginger hair, wrapped up in a bun, and green eyes. Lizzie had long brunette hair and brown eyes.

"Lizzie, you'll die," Sam told her.

"Everybody has to die at some point. Maybe it's my time," Lizzie tells him taking his hands.

"No, I don't accept that. Vikki please," Alex pleads. Vikki looks at Lizzie and then at Alex, she sighs before biting her wrist.

"Okay, for you," she tells him leaning down.

"No!" Lizzie says.

"Sorry, Lizzie," Vikki responds before shoving her wrist over Lizzie's mouth. Lizzie starts to heal. When she's finished, Alex and Sam help her up.

"We need to move and quickly. Before people find out what Vikki is," Alex says. They head towards the edge of the woods.

"Our home!" She says looking at the remains of what was there mansion. Bombs keep going off.

"Lizzie, we need to go," Alex tells her. Lizzie nods and they all head into the woods.

Back to present day.

"I know what we did was wrong, but I didn't want to lose Lizzie, I wasn't ready to," Alex says.

"I know, but we lost her anyway," Sam tells him. They sit there for a few minutes just gazing, before they get up and head off. That night Alex is tossing and turning in his sleep. Flashbacks of that night keep flowing back to him.

"Lizzie…" He keeps saying.

In his dream, he is running through the woods with Sam, Lizzie and Vikki. The sky is dusky; they have been running most of the day.

"Stop, we can't keep going," Lizzie says leaning against a tree, panting.

"She's right. We must split up. A group of us will raise suspicion," Vikki tells them. Sam nods and Alex looks between them all.

"But we're family," he says.

"I know, but it's for the best. We will meet up in three days by the wishing well. That gives us all some time to stop being hunted," Vikki replies. Alex looks at her, and walks towards her, Sam goes over to Lizzie.

"I don't want to lose you," he tells her.

"You won't. I promise," Vikki assures him she kisses him and then walks towards Lizzie.

"I'll go first," she tells them. Her and Lizzie hug. She looks at them all.

"It's been fun while it lasted. See you in three days," Vikki says before disappearing. Lizzie looks at Alex, he walks towards her.

"Sam, you go with her." Alex says.

"No," Lizzie replies. Alex puts his hand on her face.

"It's my job to protect us now. You're my little sister; I won't let anything happen to you," he tells her. He turns around to face Sam.

"Our parents aren't here now, it's up to us. We only have each other," He announces. He walks to the side with Sam.

"Take care of her," he says.

"I will, with my life," Sam replies. Alex nods. He goes back over to Lizzie to hug her goodbye.

"We'll meet again," he tells her while they hug. Just as he lets go a gunshot goes off. Lizzie falls to the ground; Sam runs over, but he gets shot too.

"Sam," Alex says. The final gunshot goes off. Alex jolts up in his bed covered in sweat. He gets up and goes to look out the window. It's dark outside and foggy.

Outside in the centre of the town, five figures emerge from the fog. Four males and one female. The girl is in the middle.

"Time to cause some chaos!" the girl says smiling. One of the lads standing next to her, looks at her and smirks.

Chapter 2
New Beginnings

The next morning, Alex is in the sitting room drinking out of a blood bag, Sam walks in.

"You look terrible, did you not sleep?" Sam asks.

"No, couldn't stop thinking about how I let Lizzie down," Alex answers.

"Alex you've got to stop beating yourself up about that. You went looking for her for years. You couldn't find her. That's not your fault," Sam tells him.

"I know, but I still can't help but feel guilty," Alex replies. Sam puts his hand on his shoulder and smiles.

"I have to head to school, but we will do something later. Try to take your mind of, off it," Sam says. Alex nods and he leaves.

In a different house, the girl from the night before walks into the living room and over to one of the boys. She slams the newspaper onto the coffee table, he looks up.

"Yes, darling sister?" He asks smiling.

"Have you read the newspaper? It says 'Greenwich is a safe place' do you know what that means? It means that you can't go biting everybody that looks tasty," she says. The boy wasn't paying attention.

"Erik, are you listening to me?" She asks. The boy known as Erik looks up.

"Relax Phoebe, I can handle this," Erik assures her. Phoebe has long, blonde hair in French braids and brown eyes. Erik has short shaggy brown hair and green eyes.

"You better," Phoebe replies. Just then, one of the other males walks in.

"You two get ready," he demands.

"What for?" Erik asks.

"School. You're both going. Erik you're pretending to be 19 and in your senior year, and Phoebe you will be 18 and in your junior year," he tells them.

"Why, Raf?" Phoebe asks.

"Because, I said so, and I'm the oldest. Now go," Rafael replies before walking off. Rafael has short light hair and was tall. Phoebe sighs before leaving and Erik follows.

At school, Mandy is in the auditorium making a list, Mia walks in.

"Hey Mand, can we talk?" She asks. Mandy puts the clipboard down and looks at her.

"What about?" She asks.

"Us, I want to apologise for my behaviour yesterday. It was rude of me and I shouldn't have said what I did," Mia tells her.

"Me too, I'm sorry. You were right, I was being mean. Brooke and Evie didn't deserve to be treated that way. I've decided to let them on the team, they were good, and we could always do with new faces," Mandy says. Mia smiles.

"Friend hug?" She asks.

"Friend hug," Mandy replies, they hug.

"Now, I have to go and greet two new students, will you post the cheer list?" Mandy asks.

"Sure," Mia replies. Mandy leaves. Erik and Phoebe walk through the school doors and look around.

"So, this is Greenwich academy. Boring!" Erik says. Phoebe side glances at him.

"Hello! You must be Erik and Phoebe. It's so nice to meet, I'm Mandy and I will be your tour guide. Follow me," Mandy says cheerily to them, she walks off.

"Mmm tasty!" Erik says to Phoebe before following.

"Erik!" Phoebe exclaims quietly, before speeding after him. Mandy finishes the tour and turns to look at them.

"Any questions?" Mandy asks.

"Yeah. Erik loves swimming, is there a team he can join?" Phoebe asks. Erik looks at her.

"Yes, the sign-up sheets will be in reception. I look forward to seeing you compete," Mandy says to him before leaving them. Phoebe laughs.

"Swimming! Really, you know I hate the water!" Erik groans. Phoebe looks at him and grins before walking away.

Taylor closes his locker door; Mia and Jake are waiting for him.

"So what? You and her are just friends again. Just like that? After yesterday?" Taylor asks confused.

"Yes, I apologised, she is my best friend," Mia reminds him.

"So were Brooke and Evie. I don't see them getting an apology," Taylor points out.

"I got them on the cheerleading team," Mia says.

"Wow Mia, do you really think that they actually want to be on the cheerleading team? They only did that to annoy

Mandy, and honestly, she deserves everything she gets," Taylor replies before walking off. Mia looks at Jake.

"What am I doing wrong?" She asks.

"Nothing really, it's just you ditched Brooke and Evie for Mandy after a lifetime of friendship and then spent two years bullying them, because it was what Mandy wanted and you haven't tried making amends since. Have you ever thought that they could be trying to get back at you guys for it?" Jake asks.

"Brooke and Evie aren't like that. They're kind and thoughtful," Mia answers.

"True but they're also hurting. How could they trust anyone when their one closest friend could ditch them so easily?" Jake replies, he kisses her on the cheek before walking off.

Sam goes into one of his classes and sits down, Phoebe nudges Erik's elbow.

"Ow!" Erik says.

"I barely touched you," Phoebe tells him.

"What was it for?" Erik asks. Phoebe points at Sam.

"Lizzie's brother," she says to him quietly. Erik looks at him and then at Phoebe.

"Wait. Who's Lizzie again?" Erik asks. Phoebe looks at him with disgust.

"Is there something wrong with your brain?" She asks.

"I don't think so," Erik answers doubtfully.

"She lived with us for fifty years," Phoebe reminds him.

"Oh Elizabeth. I remember now," Erik tells her. Sam looks at them when he hears her name.

"Stop talking, I think he heard you," Phoebe says looking away. After class, Sam approaches Phoebe and Erik in the halls. Erik smiles and Phoebe nudges him.

"How do you know my sister?" Sam asks.

"Well, uh, you see Lizzie used to live with us," Phoebe replies. Sam looks at them before handing them a piece of paper.

"This is my address. Come round tonight, we can talk then," he says before walking away. Phoebe and Erik look at each other.

After school, that day, Phoebe and Erik arrive home. Rafael is sitting on the sofa with his feet up reading a newspaper. The other two men are there to, one sitting at the table reading a book and the other standing by the window. Phoebe's grinning.

"Why are you so cheery?" The one by the window asks without even looking at her.

"It's been a good day, Nathan," Phoebe says. Nathan sniggers.

"Do you hear her Elliot? It's been a good day," he replies.

"Don't be mean Nathan," Elliot says. Nathan is muscular with short hair. Elliot has dark hair and is slim.

"Fine, go on then sister tell me. Why has it been a good day?" Nathan asks.

"We met him," Phoebe replies.

"Who?" Nathan asks.

"Sam, Lizzie's brother," Erik answers for her. Rafael looks up from the newspaper for the first time.

"Is she here? Lizzie?" He asks.

"I don't know. He invited us around tonight, to talk," Phoebe replies. Elliot slams the book shut.

"I don't think so," He declares with a raised voice.

"Why not? Don't you want to know what happened and why she did what Raf says? They could have answers. She could be there," Phoebe protests.

"I'm with Elliot. It could be a trick," Rafael says.

"Well, now I want to go," Nathan comes out with.

"You do?" Erik asks.

"Yes, anything to disobey Rafael," Nathan answers. Phoebe smiles and then walks towards Elliot.

"Please Elliot. For me? It would mean a lot, and you could finally get some peace with the truth," Phoebe points out. Elliot looks at his sister and sighs.

"Fine, for you," he says. Phoebe squeals and hugs him.

"I'll stay here," Rafael tells them.

"Suit yourself," Nathan responds, before walking out. The rest follow.

Back at Sam's, he walks through the front door.

"Alex?" He shouts. Alex appears in the room.

"What? Is something wrong?" He asks.

"I know I said that you should take your mind of Lizzie, but I met some people today. They know her," Sam replies.

"Okay," Alex says suspiciously.

"I've invited them over. I've never seen them before, which can only mean that Lizzie met them after she left us. They could know where she is and if she's alive," Sam informs him.

"And what if it's bad news?" Alex asks. The doorbell goes.

"Guess we're about to find out," Sam answers walking towards the door, Alex follows. Sam opens the door and lets them in Alex is standing in the main room waiting.

"Welcome to my house," Alex says smiling. Phoebe gets excited.

"You must be Alexander. Lizzie's oldest brother," she says.

"That would be me," Alex replies.

"Please sit down. What are your names?" Sam asks.

"I'm Phoebe. These are my brother Erik, Nathan and Elliot," Phoebe answers.

"Well, it's great to meet you, please tell me how you know my sister?" Alex asks.

"Right, of course. Lizzie lived with us," Phoebe replies.

"For how long?" Alex asks.

"50 years," Erik pipes up.

"And where is she now? Is she alive?" Alex asks.

"We don't know. She left," Nathan responds.

"What do you mean left?" Sam asks.

"Left, ran away. We weren't good enough for her anymore, so she abandoned us," Elliot breaks. He gets up and walks out slamming the door behind him.

"I'm sorry about him. He's just really upset. He was in love with Lizzie, they were engaged. It hit him harder," Phoebe tells them.

"Oh," Sam says.

"I'll go check on him. Continue," Nathan replies getting up and walking out.

"What year was this? What year did you meet my sister?" Alex asks.

"We met her in 1875 and we last saw her in 1925," Phoebe tells them.

"That was so long ago," Sam replies.

"Yeah, sorry we couldn't be more help. We were hoping you knew where she was," Phoebe informs them.

"No, we haven't seen her since 1856," Alex responds. Phoebe nods.

"We should be going. It was nice to meet you; we will let you know, if we hear anything," Phoebe tells them.

"Yeah, you too and same here, if we hear anything, we will tell you," Sam says walking them to the door. Once they've left Alex kicks the table.

"Alex, calm down," Sam declares.

"Calm down! We have nothing. We don't even know if she's alive. We let her down. So, don't tell me to calm down," Alex barks before storming out the room. Sam thinks back to the last time they saw Lizzie.

Flashback to 1855

Sam wakes up after being shot; he goes towards Lizzie who still hasn't woken up.

"She'll take longer. Vikki had been feeding us blood for three years that was Lizzie's first time. Her body isn't used to it," Alex says appearing behind him with a body. He chucks it towards Sam.

"Drink, or your transition won't be complete," he informs him. Sam drinks from the man. Lizzie wakes up and sees her brothers; they have blood dripping from their faces.

"No!" She says moving back from them. Alex wipes his mouth and approaches her.

"Lizzie, listen to me. If you don't feed, you will die," Alex tells her.

"No, I don't care. Let me die," Lizzie says to him getting up.

"You don't know what you're saying okay. You're scared and confused and that's okay, because we will help you," Alex says. Lizzie shakes her head and steps back.

"Alex," Sam says. Alex ignores him.

"I'm sorry Lizzie," he says. Lizzie goes to run, but as she turns, Alex is already there. He shoves some blood down her throat. Lizzie tries to fight him.

"No, no, no," Lizzie repeats trying to spit it out.

"It's for the best," Alex tells her.

"That wasn't your choice," Lizzie replies with tears in her eyes.

"I couldn't bear to lose you," Alex informs her.

"Too late. You've lost me," Lizzie says before disappearing.

Back to present day.

Phoebe and her brothers arrive home. Rafael is pacing in the dining room.

"Raf, what's wrong?" Phoebe asks.

"There's something I never told you guys," Rafael replies, not looking at them and still pacing.

"Rafael, stop pacing. Tell us, what is it?" Nathan asks going over to him.

"Lizzie, she well, she never left. I lied," Rafael tells them.

"What do you mean you lied? What happened to Lizzie?" Elliot barks. Rafael looks between his siblings, he sighs.

"I killed her," he says. Just then the candles go out by a strange gust of wind, the doors fly open, and Rafael goes flying through the wall.

"Raf!" Phoebe exclaims running towards him. Nathan and Erik help him up.

"Are you okay?" Erik asks.

"I'm fine," Rafael answers. He walks through the wall and stops dead in his track.

"No," he says. His siblings follow his gaze. On the other side of the table sits Lizzie with her feet up.

"Did you miss me?" Lizzie asks.

Chapter 3
Secrets Out

Rafael stares at her. "You! You're supposed to be dead!" Rafael spits out.

"Well, technically I am. We all are," Lizzie tells him. She gets up of the seat and walks towards them.

"I mean, how are you here? I killed you," Raf says.

"Well clearly you failed," Erik tells him. His family looks at him.

"You mean after you chained me to the radiator and set the place on fire?" Lizzie asks.

"Yes," Rafael replies. Lizzie smiles.

"I'm so glad you asked. Let's take a trip down memory lane," Lizzie responds.

Flashback to 1925

Lizzie wakes up chained to a radiator, smoke surrounding her. She shouts for help, but nobody hears her, she starts to struggle, trying to break free. It's of no use. The fire starts to spread rather quickly; Lizzie can hear distant screaming of the villagers. She closes her eyes and hopes for it to be over quickly. The screaming stops, she opens her eyes and realises she's no longer chained to the radiator and the fire has stopped. She gets up, confused. She looks around the room has black ash all up the walls from where the fire started to burn. She heads down what's left of the wooden staircase, the downstairs has been destroyed from where the fire started.

"Elliot," She says with worry. She heads outside, half the village has been burnt to the ground. There are bodies everywhere. Some dead, some alive. She looks around, no sign of Elliot or his family.

Back to present day.

"So, you see, your plan failed terribly. Here I am healthy and alive. Well, the most alive I can be," Lizzie tells then.

"Wait go back, I'm confused. What happened to the fire?" Erik asks.

"Oh that. Yeah, I stopped it with my mind. Pretty awesome right," Lizzie replies.

"Elizabeth Jones. I love you," Erik declares, going over and hugging her.

"Hold on a minute. That's impossible. No vampire should be able to use magic," Rafael says.

"Well, I did," Lizzie tells him.

"I don't believe you," Rafael replies. Lizzie sighs and rolls her eyes. She waves her hand, and the wall fixes itself. Rafael, Elliot and Nathan looked at her shocked. Phoebe and Erik grin.

"I missed you!" Phoebe squeals going over and hugging her.

"Me too," Lizzies responds.

"Yes, yes, yes. You all missed Lizzie!" Rafael says sourly. Lizzie pouts.

"Awe Rafael, don't be such a baby," Lizzie tells him. Rafael pulls a face at her.

"I can't believe you lied to us for all those years," Phoebe says.

"Are you really surprised?" Nathan asks her.

"Wait, what did he lie about?" Lizzie asks.

"He told us you left, because we weren't enough anymore," Erik informs her.

"Oh, that's good to know," Lizzie says.

"I'm mad," Nathan asks.

"Just say the word and I can turn him into a toad," Lizzie tells him. Nathan and Erik smile at her.

"Oh Lizzie, your brothers are here," Phoebe informs her.

"I know, that's why I came here. I finally tracked them down. You guys were a bonus," Lizzie replies.

"Have you already seen them?" Nathan asks her.

"No, I should probably go there now," Lizzie answers. She leaves.

At the Jones house, Alex and Sam walk through the front door talking. Lizzie is standing by the sofas. They stop when they see her.

"It's been a while," she says.

"A while? Try one hundred and sixty-one years. That isn't a while," Sam replies.

"I know, I'm sorry," she tells them.

"Where were you, Lizzie? We tried looking for you, but you were nowhere to be found. We didn't even know if you were alive!" Alex says with a slightly raised voice. Lizzie looks at the floor.

"It wasn't easy," she responds.

"What? Dropping of the face of the world with no trace?" Sam asks annoyed.

"Any of it! You don't know how hard it has been. I lost everything. My home, my family and then my life and if I remember rightly, you're the reason it all happened. So, forgive me, if I wasn't exactly in the mood for some family get together," Lizzie snaps.

"You're right. I am the reason you've lived longer than you wanted to, and you had every right to be mad. You needed some time alone to clear your head. That is understandable, and I'm sorry Lizzie, I really am," Alex says.

"Look, I didn't come here to argue or open up old wounds. I came here because you guys are my family and I wanted to come home. I wanted to be with you again. If you'll have me," Lizzie responds.

"If we'll, have you? Of course, we will have you. Lizzie, we have waited so long for this, but you're home. Hopefully, it's permanent," Alex says. Lizzie looks at him.

"Yes, it's permanent. I'm not going anywhere," Lizzie informs them. Alex smiles then goes over to hug her.

"Thank you," he says.

A few hours later they're sitting on the sofa catching up.

"So, you never left them?" Alex asks. Sam hands her a hot drink.

"No! Never! They were my family for fifty years. I would never just leave them," Lizzie replies.

"Are you mad?" Sam asks.

"No, honestly, I expected Rafael to lie to them. He's a little messed up," Lizzie tells him.

"No, I mean at Rafael for what he did," Sam replies.

"Oh, not anymore. I was for a long time but coming back here and seeing everyone made me realise that I've missed out on too much by being angry. It's time to let go and move on with my life," Lizzie explains.

"What if he tries again?" Sam asks. Lizzie shrugs.

"If he tries again. I'll kill him!" Alex responds. Lizzie looks at him.

"Let me show you guys something," She says taking their hands. She closes her eyes, and the room goes dark, a blue dome appears around them. It shows flashbacks of them as kids playing together. It shows them growing up and stops just before all the bad stuff happened. Lizzie opens her eyes, and the room lights up again. Her brothers look at her.

"That was really cool, do it again?" Sam says. Lizzie smiles at him.

"How'd you do that?" Alex asks.

"It's part of who we are. Our mum was a witch, it runs in our blood," Lizzie tells them.

"Then why can't we do it?" Alex asks.

"You have to activate it first," Lizzie answers.

"Okay and how would we do this?" Sam asks.

"Most witches can only activate it at a time of need. So, when I was in danger and panicked, I activated it. You guys need to do the same," Lizzie tells them.

"My life is never in danger. I'm normally the one putting other lives in danger," Sam informs her.

"Well then you might never be a witch," Lizzie tells him. He smiles.

"That's cool with me. I like my life the way it is," Sam replies. Lizzie looks at the clock.

"It's getting late. I've had a long day. We can talk some more tomorrow," she says before getting up and exiting the room.

The next morning, Rafael comes into the dining room, his family are sitting around the table. They look at him when he enters.

"Raf, we've decided to forgive you," Phoebe informs him.

"Really?" Rafael asks.

"Yes, but on one condition," Nathan answers.

"Anything. You name it, I do it," Rafael replies.

"You have to meet with Lizzie and fix it," Erik says.

"What!" Rafael says repulsed by this idea.

"You heard us. You will apologise for you actions towards her and then ensure that nothing like that will ever happen again. Then and only then we will forgive you," Elliot declares.

Rafael looks at them all and sighs. "Fine, only for you guys," he responds before leaving.

Lizzie walks into her front room and sees her brothers standing there drinking blood from the same woman. She coughs and they look up.

"Enjoying yourselves?" She asks.

"Oh yes, care to join?" Alex asks her.

"I'll pass. See you guys later," she says before walking out the front door. Alex and Sam look at each other before going back to their meal.

Lizzie heads into the bar/restaurant in town and looks around. It's a small place with a two amusement machines and a dart board next to the door. Across the room is the bar and there are a few tables spread around. "Welcome to the Joint. My name is Taylor, and I will be your waiter this morning," Taylor says appearing in front of her and holding up a menu.

Lizzie looks at him and smiles. "Hi Taylor, it's nice to meet you. I'm Lizzie," she says extending her hand. He shakes it.

"Shall I show you to a table?" He asks. Lizzie nods. Taylor takes her over to a table and hands her a menu. After she orders, Taylor leaves and Lizzie looks over at the kids playing at the amusement machines. About twenty minutes later, Taylor brings the food over and follows her gaze to the kids. "Do you want any?" Taylor asks her.

Lizzie looks at him. "It's very complicated." She tells him, Taylor hands her the food and leaves. Lizzie starts eating. Sometime later, the seat opposite her pulls out and Nathan sits down. Lizzie looks at him. "What can I help you with Nathan?" She asks.

"What makes you think I want something?" Nathan asks.

"Three reasons. Reason one, you're you. Reason two, I know you and reason three, you always want something," Lizzie informs him.

"You make a fair point," he tells her. Taylor comes over with the check. "He's paying," Lizzie says before walking out. Nathan grins, pulls out his wallet and hands Taylor a one hundred pounds. Taylor looks at him.

"Keep the rest," Nathan says before walking out after Lizzie. "So, can I tell you what I want now?" He asks catching up with her. Lizzie stops.

"Alright, what is it?" She asks.

"I would like you to meet Rafael," Nathan tells her. Lizzie looks at him.

"I've already have met him," she says.

"That's not what I mean. I would like you to meet up with him," he informs her.

"Are you out of your mind? He tried to kill me," Lizzie reminds him.

"Yes, I know, and that's why he wants to meet. He wants to make things right for his family. You were family once to love, do you remember that?" Nathan reminds her.

"I remember that ridiculous name you gave me after you made me kill a bunny. I owe you my life and that will never change," Lizzie tells him.

"Well, you're the one who started crying over it," Nathan reminds her.

"It was a bunny," Lizzie declares. Nathan smiles at her.

"Please, for us. Just hear him out?" Nathan pleads. Lizzie looks at him.

"Okay. For you guys," Lizzie says.

"Thank you!" Nathan replies before disappearing. Lizzie's phone beeps with a message of Rafael.

Lizzie arrives on the rooftop where Rafael told her to meet; he sits on the wall at the end. Lizzie looks at him. "A rooftop. Not suspicious at all," she says.

"Well, I'm a man of suspicion," Rafael replies. They look at each other for a few minutes before Rafael pats the place next to him. "Sit, let's talk," he tells her. Lizzie talks over and sits next to him. "Just to make it clear I'm only here for my family," he tells her.

"Don't worry. I'm not here for you," Lizzie replies. They sit there in silence for a minute.

"So, I guess an apology is in order," Rafael finally says. He looks at her, she notices.

"What?" She asks.

"I'm waiting," Rafael tells her.

"Seriously! Me? You're the one who tried to kill me," Lizzie reminds him.

"True, but I wouldn't have if you didn't provoke me," Rafael tells her.

"Provoke you, how? What did I do?" Lizzie asks.

Raphael pulls a face. "I'm sure I can think of something," he answers. Lizzie shakes her head and sighs.

"You are actually unbelievable," she tells him.

"Thank you," he says. Lizzie gets up and goes to walk off. Rafael grabs her arm. "Wait, please. You're right," he tells her. She stops and sits back down. "I do have something to apologise for," he replies. Lizzie looks at him. "I'm sorry that I didn't succeed," he says before pushing her of the roof. Lizzie screams, just before she hits the floor somebody catches her.

"Nice of you to drop in," The voice says, putting her down. She smiles.

"Ben," she says hugging him. He smiles back.

"The one and only," he replies before letting go. Ben is tall with dark hair and brown eyes.

"What are you doing here?" Lizzie asks.

"I was just in the neighbourhood," Ben answers. Lizzie looks at him.

"I missed you," she says.

"Me too," he replies. They stand there for a minute before Ben says, "Can we go somewhere and talk?"

"Sure, there's a place around the corner called the joint. I'll meet you there, but there's something I have to do first," she tells him. He nods before heading off.

Rafael arrives home smiling to himself; he goes into the dining room where Phoebe, Erik and Nathan sit. "How did it go?" Phoebe asks.

"It went good. Where's Elliot?" Rafael asks.

"Upstairs," Erik replies. Nathan leans forward looking at him.

"So, what happened?" He queries. Rafael goes to answer but doesn't get the chance. He gets thrown against the wall and Lizzie shoves her hand into his chest. Rafael grins.

"Give me one good reason why I shouldn't rip your heart out right now," Lizzie asks him.

"Because you're not like him, like us. You never have been. You don't kill people, you're good. You save them and you never give up," Elliot replies entering the room. He walks towards her and places his hand on her arm. "Let him go Lizzie," he says. Lizzie looks between them.

"You're not worth it anyway," she tells him letting go.

"Lizzie, what happened?" Phoebe asks.

"What happened is Rafael tried to kill me, again. After telling me that I should apologise," Lizzie answers. His family look at him, he shrugs.

"Well, I say let her. Good riddance," Erik says. Phoebe clips the back of his head.

"Come on Lizzie, let's go for a walk." Elliot says. Lizzie looks at him.

"I have plans," she replies leaving.

Lizzie arrives at the joint and walks towards Ben, who's sitting at the bar. He looks up and smiles at her. "Did you sort out your business?" He asks.

"Yeah," Lizzie replies, she sits down next to him on a barstool.

"What was it?" He asks.

"Just something from my past, don't worry about it," Lizzie answers.

"Always with the secrets," he says. Lizzie smiles at him.

"So, what are you doing here?" Lizzie asks.

"Just passing through, you know me always on the move," Ben tells her.

"Well, that's a shame," she says.

"Really?" Ben asks.

"Yeah, I'd be upset if you left again," Lizzie informs him. Taylor appears behind the bar.

"Hey Lizzie," he says.

"Hey Taylor, what's up?" Lizzie asks.

"Nothing, but can you tell your friend from earlier that he is welcome round here anytime," Taylor replies.

"Sure," Lizzie says. Elliot comes through the door.

"Ooh, a tall and handsome stranger just walked through the door." Taylor informs her. Lizzie turns around.

"Elliot," she says, Ben follows her gaze.

"Go, I'll be fine," he tells her.

"Are you sure?" She asks.

"Yes, go." Ben replies. Lizzie smiles at him.

"Thank you," she says, she gets up and kisses him on the cheek.

"It was good to see you," Ben informs her.

"You too, hopefully I'll see you again," Lizzie replies before walking away. She leaves with Elliot. Ben watches them.

"Man, why did you let her leave?" Taylor asks. Ben turns to look at him.

"What?" He asks.

"I'm no expert, but I can tell when two people have feelings for each other," Taylor says.

"Oh no, we don't," Ben tries to explain. Taylor just looks at him and Ben sighs. "She loves him," he tells Taylor.

"Maybe, but something tells me they won't last long. Besides just because you love someone doesn't mean you can't catch feelings for someone else," Taylor informs him.

"He's better for her. I can't make her happy, I'm not staying," Ben replies.

"Perhaps you should. Your feelings for her won't change overnight. If you go, you will miss out. You deserve the chance to make her happy too; don't let some other guy be the one," Taylor warns him before walking away.

Lizzie and Elliot are walking through the woods.

"So, how have things been?" Lizzie asks him. Elliot looks at her.

"It's been 91 years since we last seen each other, and that's the first thing you ask?" Elliot says.

"Yes?" Lizzie replies. He smiles.

"Okay, well things have been good. It got better when I saw you, but overall, I've been good," Elliot tells her. They come to the end of the woods and stop.

"So, nothing interesting has happened to you?" Lizzie asks.

"No, interesting only happens when you're around," Elliot tells her. He steps closer. A car pulls up next to them and a woman gets out.

"Elliot!" She says. Elliot looks at her.

"Heather," he says surprised. Lizzie looks between them.

"I'm sorry, who are you?" She asks. Heather looks at her.

"I'm his fiancé," she replies.

Chapter 4
Broken Hearts

The next morning Lizzie comes downstairs with a bag, she grabs her jacket. "Where are you going?" Alex asks.

"School. It's my first day," Lizzie reminds him. Sam comes out of the next room.

"Would it kill you to smile?" He asks her. Lizzie pulls a face at him. Sam grabs his shoes, and the door knocks, Lizzie gets it.

"Ben!" She says when she sees him. He smiles.

"Want to go for a walk?" He asks. She nods and leaves with him. They walk for a little bit before Ben speaks.

"I decided to listen to you and stay," he informs her.

"Really, that's great," Lizzie replies.

"Yeah, so what happened with you and Elliot?" Ben asks. Lizzie looks at him.

"So, let me get this straight. You got engaged to this person and never told us?" Phoebe asks Elliot. She's sitting at the dining table with Erik. Elliot stands opposite them with Heather. Nathan and Rafael are standing near the door.

"Yes, and her name is…"

"Heather," Lizzie tells Ben.

"Wow, that's shocking," Ben says. Lizzie nods.

"Wait, aren't you still engaged to Lizzie?" Erik asks.

"They haven't seen each other in years. They can't still be engaged," Rafael replies.

"Of course, you would say that," Nathan responds.

"I guess it has been over 90 years. He deserves to move on," Lizzie tells Ben.

"Are you okay with that?" Ben asks.

"I have to be," Lizzie replies.

"Look I never thought I would see Lizzie again, I was alone. Then I met Heather, she gave me hope and she made me happy," Elliot tells them.

"I know it must come as a shock. Elliot told me how you all felt about Lizzie. I'm not trying to replace her; I just want a chance to prove that I can make him happy too," Heather tells them.

"Oh, jeez, lucky us." Phoebe says sarcastically.

"Phoebe please, for me?" Elliot says. She sighs and gets up.

"I'm going out tonight with some friends from school. You can come if you want. You have one chance to impress me and it's not easy," She says before walking out. Erik follows.

"Ignore her; she's just trying to make you leave. I am glad you're here. It's about time we get another sister," Rafael says.

"Thank you," Heather replies. Elliot looks at Nathan.

"Welcome to the family," he says before walking off.

Ben and Lizzie stop.

"We are, at school," Ben says looking across the road.

"Thanks," Lizzie replies.

"Why are you in school? You're twenty-five," Ben queries. Lizzie smiles.

"I guess I wanted to make the most out of my new life. I never got to go to school before," Lizzie answers.

"So how old does everyone think you are?" He asks.

"Nineteen. Sam and I are pretending to be twins," Lizzie responds.

"Well then, have a good day, I guess," Ben tells her. He turns around.

Lizzie enters the school and Sam appears.

"Thanks for waiting," he says to her.

"Sorry, I forgot," Lizzie tells him.

"Yeah, I know. Anyway, lets' get you signed in," he replies. They head towards an office door and Lizzie goes in. About ten minutes later, she comes out.

"So, how'd it go?" Sam asks.

"The head teacher is extremely intimidating," Lizzie replies. Sam nods.

"We have lesson," he tells her.

"Yeah, let me just go to my locker and I'll meet you there," Lizzie replies.

"Okay, don't get lost," Sam responds before walking away. Lizzie heads over to her locker and opens it.

"Hey, I didn't know you would be here," Taylor says walking towards her.

"Yeah, I started today," Lizzie replies.

"Cool, which lesson do you have first?" Taylor asks.

"Science, but I'm late," she tells him.

"Don't worry; it's your first day," Taylor says.

"Why aren't you in lesson?" Lizzie asks.

"I'm late, but the good news is I have science too. Shall we be late together?" He asks holding his arm out, Lizzie smiles.

"We shall," She replies taking his arm. They walk off together. They arrive at the classroom and go in.

"You're late!" The teacher says as they walk in.

"Sorry Miss, the head teacher asked me to wait for the new student," Taylor replies pointing at Lizzie.

"Oh, okay then. You must be Elizabeth, welcome to my science class. Take a seat next to Erik," The teacher says. Lizzie nods and walks towards the table; Erik sits there grinning at her. An hour later, the bell goes, and everyone gets up. Lizzie leaves with Erik and Phoebe.

"I'm so glad you're here!" Phoebe says to Lizzie.

"Why?" She asks.

"Erik can be annoying," Phoebe tells her.

"You're just say that cause you're his sister. He's not all that bad, you know," Lizzie says. Phoebe shrugs. They head into the library.

"Lizzie," Sam says going over with two people.

"Sam, what's up?" Lizzie asks.

"I would like to introduce you to my friends. This is Evie and Brooke. Guys this is my twin, Elizabeth," Sam introduces them.

"Hi, it's so nice to meet you," Evie responds. Lizzie smiles.

"Hey, so we're going out clubbing tonight. You guys should come," Phoebe says.

"Really?" Brooke asks.

"Sure, you're old enough right?" Phoebe answers.

"Yeah, were both nineteen," Evie tells her.

"Great, we'll see you there," Erik says unenthusiastically walking off. Lizzie looks at Phoebe.

"I'll catch up with you guys later," she tells everyone before leaving. She catches up with Erik.

"Hey, what's going on. Are you okay?" Lizzie asks him.

"Yeah," Erik replies.

"Would you like to try again. Maybe make it sound believable," Lizzie responds. Erik sighs and stops. He looks at her.

"If I tell you, will you not repeat anything?" Erik asks her.

"Erik, I would never tell anyone anything. You know that," Lizzie tells him.

"Okay, Elliot has a new fiancée and Rafael is loving it. Phoebe and Nathan are not, and I am stuck in the middle. My house is turning into a warzone and I do not know whose side I should be on. Phoebe's pretending everything fines. Elliot is just moving on with his life. Rafael is getting away with everything and Nathan has become a nutcase. They can barely look at each other, I don't feel like we're a family anymore and I don't know what to do," Erik tells her. Lizzie looks at him.

"Well, I don't know what to say. Your family has never been normal. You know you guys all work in a unique way. It has always been Rafael and Phoebe, Nathan and Elliot. You were always alone, trying to keep the whole family together. If Elliot has found someone that makes him happy, then maybe you should be happy for him. You don't have to take sides Erik; you should just do what makes you happy. Put yourself first, maybe try distancing yourself and let them go to each other, instead of you trying to fix them," Lizzie suggests.

"Or maybe we just need you," Erik says.

"Me?" Lizzie asks.

"Yeah, Lizzie you've always been the glue. We were fine for that time you lived with us and we fell apart when you left. It's easy to tell that your brothers were lost without you and I know you're going to make new friends here that will only be together because of you," Erik tells her. Lizzie looks at him. "Erik, I can't. I can't be everyone's saviour," Lizzie replies. Erik looks at the floor disappointed. Lizzie looks at him. "Come here," she says hugging him, he hugs her back. "I'm always going to be on your side," she tells him before letting go and walking away.

Later that evening, Lizzie is in her bedroom, a stone hits her window. She goes over to the window and opens it. She sees Ben standing there smiling. He takes a step back and runs up. He jumps up to the window.

"What are you doing?" Lizzie asks.

"I just wanted to see you," Ben answers.

"We have a front door," Lizzie reminds him. Ben shrugs.

"I'd rather use the window," Ben responds. He comes in and closes the window. "Nice room," he says looking around. He looks at Lizzie and notices she's dressed up.

"Do you have plans?" He asks.

"Oh, Phoebe has made plans to go to a club tonight. She asked me to come," Lizzie replies.

"Well, you look great," Ben tells her. Lizzie smiles.

"Thanks, would you like to come?" Lizzie asks.

"I don't know, clubbing is not my thing," Ben answers.

"Maybe, but I would like you there," Lizzie tells him. Ben walks towards her and brushes some hair from her face.

"How are you?" He asks her.

"What?" She asks.

"How do you feel, about this whole Elliot thing?" Ben asks her.

"Oh, I'm fine. I'm not even thinking about it," Lizzie answers. Ben looks into her eyes. He holds her gaze for a minute before stepping back.

"Have a good night," he tells her before walking back towards the window and disappearing.

Lizzie arrives at the club with Sam and sees Phoebe, Erik, Brooke and Taylor there. She heads over to the table.

"Hey guys, who are we waiting for?" She asks.

"Evie, Jake and Heather," Phoebe answers with an unapproved tone on her name. Sam looks at Erik.

"Who's Heather?" He asks.

"It's a long story," Erik tells him. Sam nods as Evie and Jake arrive.

"Let's start," Phoebe says. She heads to the bar and comes back a few minutes later with a tray of shots. Erik pulls Phoebe over to him and Sam.

"Phoebe, you remember that we can't get drunk," Erik asks her quietly.

"Why?" Sam asks.

"Because they're half werewolves," Lizzie tells him going over.

"Oh, that sucks to be you," Sam says. He heads over to the table and sits with Evie. He picks up a shot.

"Are you not drinking?" Phoebe asks Jake.

"No, I'm not a drinker," Jake answers.

"Suit yourself," she says picking up a shot. After a while, Lizzie heads over to the bar.

"Enjoying yourself?" Someone asks. She looks behind her.

"Vikki," Lizzie says. They hug.

"I missed you," Vikki tells her.

"Not as much as I've missed you," Lizzie replies. Vikki looks over towards the table.

"So, who are your friends?" She asks.

"Some of them are old friends and others I met today at school," Lizzie tells her.

"You're twenty-five years old. Why do you go to school?" Vikki asks.

"We look young enough, and it's a nice change," Lizzie responds.

"Makes sense," Vikki says. Sam looks over and sees her. Vikki waves. He gets up and goes over.

"Now there's a ghost from the past," Sam says hugging her.

"I've been bored without you too Sam," she tells him.

"What are you doing here?" Sam asks grinning from head to toe.

"Well, I found out you guys were here. I came back for you," Vikki replies.

"Have you seen Alex. He has missed you so bad," Sam tells her.

"Where is he?" Vikki asks. Sam tells her the address and she leaves.

"Are you coming?" Sam asks her as he walks towards the table.

"In a minute. I'm just going bathroom," Lizzie answers. She heads the opposite away. When she comes out, she bumps into someone.

"Ben," she says surprised. He looks at her.

"I decided to come. I wanted to see you," Ben tells her.

"I'm glad you did. It was starting to get boring," Lizzie replies. Ben smiles.

"Should we go out and join everyone?" He asks.

"Yeah," Lizzie answers. They head out and start walking towards the table. They stop, sitting at the table with everyone is Heather and Elliot. They look happy together. Ben looks at Lizzie.

"Lizzie, are you okay?" He asks.

"I lied. I'm not fine," she answers. Ben lets out a breath.

"Come on, I'll take you home," Ben tells her placing his hand on her back and leading her out.

Later that night, Ben is sitting on the roof, Lizzie walks over and joins him.

"Hey, how do you feel?" Ben asks as she sits next to him.

"Better thanks. The bath was nice and refreshing," Lizzie answers. He smiles at her.

"You know, I never thought I'd see you again after I saved your life," he tells her.

"Why?" Lizzie asks.

"I don't know. You and your friend disappeared. I thought that was it, you were gone, and I missed my chance," Ben replies.

"Your chance? Chance for what?" Lizzie asks. Ben looks at her.

"Just to have you in my life," he replies. Lizzie nods.

"Okay, to be honest I felt the same way. It has been forty years. I didn't think I'd see you again," Lizzie responds.

"What happened with your friend?" Ben asks.

"Vikki? We went our separate ways, but she's back now," Lizzie answers.

"It looks like everyone's back together," Ben tells her. She looks at him and smiles.

"I'm glad you decided to stay. You're somebody I never want to lose," Lizzie informs him.

"I never want to lose you either," Ben responds. Lizzie rests her head on his shoulder.

Chapter 5
The Truth

The next day Lizzie is sitting at the bar in The Joint talking to Taylor.

"Where'd you go last night?" Taylor asks.

"I bumped into Ben and we left," Lizzie answers.

"Is Ben joining our school?" Taylor asks.

"I don't think so, why?" Lizzie asks.

"We're all nineteen and you and he are good friends. He's about our age, just thought he'd be in school," Taylor asks.

"He's older than us," Lizzie answers.

"How much older?" Taylor asks.

"Three years," Lizzie replies.

"You must have a thing for older guys. I met Elliot last night and he's twenty-eight," Taylor says. Lizzie looks at the glass of water in her hand.

"Do you have anything stronger?" She asks Taylor.

"Yeah, but don't you think it's a little early to start drinking. It's only four in the afternoon," Taylor replies.

"It's never too early," Lizzie tells him. Taylor walks over to the shelves.

"Okay, we have vodka, gin, bourbon, whiskey, tequila, brandy, rum basically anything," Taylor informs her.

"I'll have some vodka," Lizzie says. Taylor picks up the bottle and a glass and goes over to her. He unscrews the lid. Lizzie takes the bottle.

"Thanks," she says drinking it. Taylor puts the glass away.

"So, I'm just going to take a wild observation and say that this has something to do with Elliot," Taylor responds.

"Correct," Lizzie says.

"What happened between you both?" Taylor asks.

"We were engaged, and we were happy, but his brother had other plans. He didn't like me, so he got rid of me. I guess Elliot just moved on," Lizzie responds.

"Hold on, back up. You guys were engaged? But you're so young," Taylor tells her. Lizzie looks at him.

"It wasn't a long engagement. Only lasted six months," Lizzie says.

"How long were you together?" Taylor asks.

"Three years. I fell for him hard. I honestly thought I'd spend the rest of my life with him," Lizzie answers.

"What about Ben?" Taylor asks.

"What about him?" Lizzie asks confused. Taylor looks at her and realises she doesn't know.

"What has he said about it, you guys seem close," Taylor says.

"Nothing, really. He's been supportive and he is so sweet and caring. Sometimes I feel like there's something he isn't telling me," Lizzie informs him.

"Maybe you should speak to him," Taylor suggests. Lizzie shrugs.

"Maybe," She speaks.

"Can I ask you something?" Taylor asks.

"Sure," Lizzie replies.

"You were only seventeen when you got with Elliot and he was twenty-five. What were your brothers like?" Taylor asks.

"They didn't know," Lizzie answers. Taylor looks at her and smiles.

"A secret relationship. They never last," He says.

"Tell me about it," Lizzie says taking another swig from the bottle.

Three hours later Lizzie is playing darts with people in the bar. Nathan walks in.

"Nathan, come join me," Lizzie says going over to him.

"In a minute," he tells her, he heads over to the bar and looks at Taylor.

"How many drinks has she had?" He asks. Taylor pulls up four empty bottles and Nathan pulls a disappointed face.

"I'll pay for it," he says getting his wallet out and handing Taylor a load of money. He looks across the room at Lizzie who is dancing with random guys.

"You should probably get her home," Taylor speaks.

"I know," Nathan responds before getting up and walking over to her, he gently grabs her arm.

"Come on love, let's take a walk," he says leading her outside.

They're walking down the road; Lizzie has Nathan's leather jacket on.

"What do you think of Heather?" Lizzie asks him.

"She's alright," Nathan replies.

"Just alright," Lizzie says. Nathan looks at her.

"Is that what this is about?" He asks.

"I know it probably sounds stupid. I haven't seen Elliot in just over ninety years and here I am, getting drunk because he's moved on," Lizzie says.

"I don't think it's stupid. I think it's natural. Just because we are vampires doesn't mean we can't be emotional. It keeps our human side alive. The fact that you're hurt over it just means that your normal," Nathan tells her. Lizzie looks at him and smiles.

"I guess it's only fair someone else gets to be with him. I was with him for forty-seven years. That's a long time," Lizzie speaks. Nathan smiles. They arrive at Lizzies house half an hour later. They stop outside it.

"Thanks Nathan, for walking me home," Lizzie says.

"Don't mention it. Go get some sleep," Nathan responds.

"You too," Lizzie replies. She goes through the front door. Sam and Alex are slouched on a sofa each and Vikki is standing up near the window. She looks over at Lizzie and sees something wrong.

"Lizzie, what is it?" Vikki asks concerned. Sam and Alex look over at her.

"Nothing, I'm fine," Lizzie tells them.

"You have a guest," Alex says.

"Who?" Lizzie asks.

"Ben, he's in your room. Tell him there's a door if he ever feels like using it. That's the reason we have it," Alex responds. Lizzie heads up the stairs, she opens her door and sees Ben standing near the window.

"How long have you been here?" She asks.

"About ten minutes," Ben answers.

"You used the window again?" She asks.

"Yeah," Ben says.

"My brother said we have door for a reason." Lizzie informs him, he grins.

"How's your day been?" He asks.

"It's been good. I was with Taylor," she answers. Ben nods, Lizzie takes of the jacket, chucks it over the chair and sits on the bed. She pats the place next to her.

"I know there's something you're not telling me, and I want you to know that you can tell me anything," Lizzie says. Ben looks at her.

"I know, I'm just not ready to tell you. I don't want to ruin this," Ben tells her. Lizzie looks into his eyes.

"You could never ruin this. You mean too much," she tells him. Ben moves closer to her and takes her hands in his.

"Lizzie, trust me. You wouldn't look at me the same. It would either make things awkward or ruin things over time," he informs her. Lizzie looks at him before leaning in and kissing him. She pulls back.

"I like you too," she whispers in his ear. She gets up and walks towards the draws. Ben gets up and walks over as she turns around. He kisses her and then moves back; he puts his head against hers.

"I want to be with you, but not like this. You're still upset over Elliot and I don't want it to feel like you're only with me to hurt him. When we do get together, I want it to be the right time, for both of us," Ben says. He kisses her on the head and then disappears.

Monday morning Lizzie is walking down the corridor at school, she bumps into Taylor.

"Hey," she says.

"Hey, how are you?" He asks.

"I'm okay," Lizzie tells him.

"Good, you had me a little worried," he replies.

"Can I ask you something?" She asks him as they head down the corridor together.

"Sure," Taylor answers.

"What can you tell me about Evie?" Lizzie asks.

"She's alright. Definitely the best out of the three of them," Taylor tells her.

"Three. I thought it was her and Brooke," Lizzie says.

"Now, but before there were three of them," Taylor says.

"What's wrong with the other two?" Lizzie asks.

"Mia is posh and rude. Brooke is loud and obnoxious. Evie is nice and quiet," Taylor informs her. They head into their science class; Lizzie goes and joins Erik. After class, Lizzie heads into the canteen and sits down at a table. Phoebe goes over and joins her.

"Hey," Lizzie says. Phoebe smiles at her and hands her an envelope.

"What's this?" Lizzie asks.

"An invitation for you and your family. Heather is so great, she let me plan her engagement party. It's on Friday night," Phoebe answers excitedly. Lizzie looks at the invite and puts it down. Phoebe hangs her head.

"I'm sorry Lizzie, that was so inconsiderate of me. Of course, you don't have to come," Phoebe tells her.

"No, it's fine. I'll be there," Lizzie replies. Phoebe lets out a little squeal and gets up. She stops and looks at Lizzie.

"Is that Nathans jacket?" She asks. Lizzie nods and Phoebe leaves. Lizzie sighs and picks up the invitation again. Lizzie grabs her stuff and gets up.

Evie is walking down the corridor; she hears voices in the girl's bathroom. She walks towards the door and opens it a little and sees her brother Ethan, with Sam.

"Let me help you, I can heal it," Sam says.

"How?" Ethan asks. Sam bites his wrist and shoves it over Ethan's mouth. His head heals, Evie gasps and closes the door slowly stepping back. She turns to run the opposite way. Sam appears in front of her.

"Hello, Evie," he says smiling. Lizzie comes round the corner.

"Once again Sam, you have reached first place for being the creepiest person alive," Lizzie tells him.

"Shush Lizzie," Sam says.

"Did you just shush me?" Lizzie asks repulsed.

"It's going down," Erik says appearing out of nowhere. Everyone stares at him.

"What?" He asks.

"Stop talking," Phoebe answers.

"Can somebody please explain what is going on?" Evie asks.

"Explain what? We don't know what happened," Lizzie responds.

"Well Sam was in the girl's toilet," Evie starts. Lizzie looks at Sam.

"What have you been told about going in the girl's toilet?" Lizzie asks him smiling.

"Wait, he's done this before?" Erik asks.

"All the time," Lizzie tells him.

"Ssh, I want to hear what happened next," A voice says from the boy's toilet.

"Taylor, is that you?" Erik asks in a seductive way. Taylor comes out as Phoebe puts her hand over Erik's mouth. He bites her.

"Ow, Erik don't bite," Phoebe says.

"Erik, you're not an animal," Lizzie speaks. Ethan comes out the girl's toilet. Everyone looks at Sam.

"Kinky," Taylor pipes up.

"Evie, it's a miracle," Ethan says to her.

"What is?" Phoebe asks.

"I fell over and smashed my head. There was blood everywhere, now it's all gone. Like it never happened. I don't even remember going into the girl's toilet," Ethan informs her.

"It was him! I saw him heal you with his blood," Evie responds.

"What!" Lizzie, Phoebe and Erik exclaim.

"How is that even possible?" Ethan asks.

"Don't worry, I can make this all go away. I can make you forget," Sam tells them both.

"I don't want to forget, you weirdo," Evie says.

"Finally, someone who agrees with me," Lizzie says. Erik grabs Ethan's face and looks him in the eyes.

"You will forget what happened today," Erik says creepily. Phoebe smacks his hand away and Ethan walks off.

"Wicked, you guys are vampires," Jake says walking towards them.

"What are vampires?" Taylor asks.

"You know those grizzly things that go grr," Erik answers.

"You're describing a bear," Phoebe tells him.

"This isn't a discussion we should be having right now. Everyone come over later, we can talk more there," Lizzie tells them. She looks at Sam, he walks towards Evie.

"You won't remember anything until you arrive at mine later," Sam says.

"Everyone, get to lesson, now!" The principal yells coming around the corner. Everyone scatters.

After school, Lizzie arrives home with Jake, Taylor, Phoebe and Erik.

"What's going on?" Alex asks. He is sitting with Vikki. Ben is there too.

"I'll let Sam explain," Lizzie tells him.

"Where is Sam?" Vikki asks. Lizzie shrugs. The door knocks and Lizzie answers it. Rafael is standing there with Nathan, Elliot and Heather.

"What do you want?" Lizzie asks Rafael.

"That's no way to speak to your guests," Rafael says walking past her. Lizzie moves back and the rest come in.

"Nice jacket," Nathan says as he walks past her.

"Phoebe messaged and said meet here," Elliot responds. Lizzie goes too close the door and it hits someone, she pulls it back and sees Sam.

"Sorry," she says pulling an apologetic face at him. Sam walks through with Evie.

"Wait," Evie says as soon as the door closes. They all look at her.

"I remember everything. You! You're dangerous," she declares looking at Sam.

"What's going on?" Alex asks sternly standing up.

"Sam let his secret spill this morning," Lizzie informs him. Alex glares at Sam.

"What were you thinking?" He asks.

"I didn't mean too. Her brother hurt himself. I was just trying to help, Evie accidentally saw it," Sam answers.

"Because you were in the girl's bathroom," Lizzie reminds him. Sam pulls a face at her.

"Okay enough. I'm sure you have some questions," Alex says to Evie. She nods.

"Wait, hold up. Why don't you just erase her memories?" Rafael asks.

"Because if she keeps them now, it could save her finding out again in the future," Erik tells him.

"Or she could tell somebody and cause us problems. If you are not going to erase her memories, there are other methods. For instance, I'm hungry," Rafael replies. He bares his teeth and walks towards her. Lizzie rolls her eyes.

"Dolor," she says looking at him. Rafael grabs his head and falls to the floor crying out in pain.

"Lizzie!" Elliot says. She just ignores him. Rafael's nose starts bleeding.

"Lizzie, come on. That's enough," Alex tells her. He gently grabs her arm. She looks at him and Rafael stops.

"It was worth it," she tells him. Rafale gets up off the floor and looks at her.

"You'll pay for that!" He warns her stepping closer to her. As soon as he does, Alex, Sam, Ben, Erik and Nathan all snarl at him. He takes a step back and holds his hands up.

"Guys! We have more important things to worry about," Vikki points out.

"Of course, why are they here though?" Nathan asks looking at Jake and Taylor.

"They were there when she found out," Phoebe tells him.

"Yeah, and Jake knew we were vampires," Sam says. Everyone looks at him.

"How?" Alex asks. Jake sighs.

"I'm a werewolf," Jake informs them.

"You are?" Taylor asks.

"This should be fun," Erik says. Jake looks at Taylor.

"I'm sorry I never told you. It's supposed to be kept a secret, for our safety," Jake tells him.

"How long have you known?" Nathan asks him.

"Three years," Jake replies.

"Wait a minute. I'm so confused," Taylor speaks. "Can somebody please explain what is going on?" He asks.

"Of course. Sit down," Lizzie tells him. She walks past him and sits next to him on the sofa.

"Do you trust me?" She asks.

"Yes," he answers. Lizzie nods and touches his head.

"Ostendit illi," she says as she closes her eyes and Taylor's shut too. After a few minutes, their eyes open and Lizzie removes her hands.

"What just happened?" Heather asks Elliot.

"I showed him the truth. Our past. What we all are. It's easier to understand way," Lizzie responds without looking at her. She gets up and walks over to the bookshelf she grabs a book and goes to the table next to the banister, opening it.

"What is that?" Jake asks.

"Spells," Lizzie answers.

"Oh, that's nice," Jake says. Evie goes and sits opposite Taylor.

"Let me see if I have this correct. Sam, his sister and brother are vampires," Evie starts.

"So are Vikki and Ben," Alex says.

"I'm also a witch," Lizzie reminds her.

"Right, Jake is a werewolf," Evie says. She looks at the other family.

"And you guys are, vampires?" She asks them unsure.

"Hybrids to be exact. Half vampire, half werewolf," Nathan informs her.

"Okay. That's not at all life changing," Evie says.

"Look, I don't want to scare you but what you've been told today has to stay between us. You cannot tell anybody else. And if you do, then we'll have to kill you," Nathan tells them.

"Noted," Taylor replies. Evie nods.

"Okay great. Well, it is getting late. We should be heading home," Nathan says to his family. He walks towards the door and leaves. His family follow, Taylor gets up.

"I guess we'll see you tomorrow," he says to Lizzie, she nods at him. Him, Jake and Evie leave. Lizzie looks at Ben.

"Where are you staying?" She asks him.

"At a hotel," Ben replies.

"You can stay here if you'd like. We have the room," Lizzie tells him. He smiles at her. Alex coughs and Lizzie looks at him.

"Is that okay with you?" She asks. Alex looks at Ben.

"Make sure you use the door from now on," Alex responds before heading upstairs. Vikki follows him. Lizzie goes and sits on the sofa, Ben and Sam join her.

Chapter 6
Engagement Party

Two days later Lizzie is in her room, Ben knocks on the door and walks in.

"Hey," Lizzie says looking at him.

"Hey, what's the dress for?" Ben asks looking across the room at the red dress sitting on her foot on. Lizzie looks at him and opens her top draw. She hands him the invitation.

"You're going to their engagement party?" Ben asks.

"Yeah, to show my support," Lizzie answers.

"But are you okay with this?" Ben asks.

"I'll be fine. They seem happy and that's all that matters. Besides, you know me, any excuse to dress up and I'm sold," Lizzie answers.

"That's true," Ben says. Lizzie looks at him.

"Are you going to come?" She asks.

"No, I'm just going to hang here tonight," Ben tells her. Lizzie goes to say something when Vikki walks in.

"Hey Ben, can I speak to Lizzie for a minute?" She asks.

"Sure," Ben says. He leaves, Vikki closes the door behind him. She walks over to the dress and picks it up.

"Are you sure tonight is a good idea? Just think about it, it's literally a night about them. Everyone will be talking about them; they'll be together, and you don't want to accidentally say or do something you'll regret," Vikki tells her.

"If I don't go, it will look like I have a problem with it. Like I can't move past him," Lizzie says.

"But you can't. You were trying to find ways to curse her last week," Vikki reminds her. Lizzie looks at her.

"I'm over it. Yes, it hurts and maybe it always will but there's no way I'm going to sit around mopping about it. I have the chance to start fresh, have a life here with new people. I can't let my past define me or stop me from having a that. If he's happy, I'm happy," Lizzie says. Vikki looks at her for a minute.

"Okay. I believe you," Vikki responds. She hands her the dress and walks towards the door. She stops and looks back at her.

"Have fun tonight," she says before leaving.

Later that night Lizzie walks towards the doors of the town hall. Her dress is long and thick with red straps coming off the shoulder.

"Lizzie," A voice shouts from behind. She turns around and sees Sam and Alex standing at the bottom of the stairs.

"What are you guys doing here?" She asks.

"Well, the invitation was for all of us," Alex replies.

"And we though you might like some company," Sam responds. They walk up and stand on either side of her and extend their arms.

"Shall we?" Alex asks. She takes them and the doors open. They walk through. They look around the room, there are so many people. Waiters are walking around with trays of champagne. On the far side of the room, Heather and Elliot stand talking to people. Heather is wearing a white dress with her hair up in a bun. Her dress is long and thin with one strap on the shoulder and the other one missing. They look across the room and notice Lizzie and the boys. They head over.

"Hi, thank you for coming," Heather says excitedly.

"Thank you for inviting us," Alex responds.

"The party looks amazing," Sam tells them.

"Thank you, I think Phoebe was a bit excited. Please help yourself to anything," Elliot says before walking away to greet new guests with Heather. Nathan walks over and holds out his hand.

"Hello love, care to dance with me?" He asks. Lizzie takes his hand, and they head into the ballroom.

"I have a favour to ask," Nathan tells her as they start dating.

"Of course, you do," Lizzie responds. Nathan looks at her.

"I wouldn't ask if it wasn't important," he says.

"What do you need?" Lizzie asks.

"Just a spell," he answers.

"What sort of spell?" Lizzie asks. Nathan sighs like he's unsure to say anything.

"Heather told us not to say anything, but I fear it could be serious," Nathan replies.

"Nathan, what is it?" Lizzie asks worried.

"They have a son. Heather and Elliot. He's twelve. There's something wrong with him. He's recently started having trouble breathing, he can barely walk, and he sometimes says he can't see anything," Nathan tells her. Lizzie looks at him.

"A son?" She asks.

"Yeah, his name is Henry," Nathan says. Lizzie goes to ask him something when Nathan spins her out and into a different partner.

"Mind if I cut in?" Elliot asks appearing behind her.

"Not at all," Lizzie answers. They start dancing, she looks at him.

"You have a son, when were you going to mention it?" She asks him.

"Soon. I just didn't feel like it was the right time. Not with everything that's happened recently," Elliot tells her.

"There never would have been a right time," Lizzie says.

"Are you mad?" Elliot asks. Lizzie looks into his eyes.

"No, I'm not. What's wrong with him?" Lizzie queries.

"What?" He asks.

"Nathan told me what was happening," Lizzie answers.

"He shouldn't have. Heather didn't want to ask you for help, she thinks you hate her," Elliot responds. Lizzie chuckles.

"I don't hate Heather. She fell in love and who could blame her. I know what that feels like," Lizzie replies. Heather rushes over to him.

"Sorry to interrupt. Elliot it's urgent," she says with a panicked tone. Elliot looks at Lizzie before rushing off with Heather. They head upstairs. Lizzie sighs before following. Heather and Elliot head into a room where Rafael, Erik and Phoebe are. It's a dull room, Rafael is sitting on a sofa with a child who is coughing up blood.

"Henry, what happened?" Elliot asks. Heather sits next to her son.

"I don't know. He just started and he won't stop. I think he's dying," Rafael tells his brother. Lizzie enters the room, and everyone looks at her.

"What are you doing here?" Rafale asks with an aggressive tone. Lizzie rolls her eyes.

"Somnum," she says and waves her hand Rafael falls to the floor with a thud. Phoebe goes over to him.

"He's fine, just sleeping," Lizzie tells her. She looks over at the sofa where Heather is sitting cradling her son, covered in blood. She walks towards them.

"What happened?" She asks.

"We don't know. One minute he was fine and the next he was coughing and had a fever," Heather informs her. Lizzie bends down in front of the child. She puts her hand on his forehead, he stops coughing. Lizzie closes her eyes, Elliot grabs Heather and moves her away. Lizzie opens her eyes and looks at Elliot and Heather.

"He's been cursed," she tells them.

"What? By whom?" Heather asks.

"I don't know. I didn't even know there was another witch in town," Lizzie answers.

"Who would want to curse a child?" Erik asks.

"That's the question," Lizzie says to him.

"Can you help him?" Elliot asks.

"Yes, I can remove the curse," Lizzie replies. Heather sighs and Lizzie looks at them.

"What?" Elliot asks.

"I might need a few things," she tells him.

"Anything," Elliot responds. Lizzie gives him a list and he leaves.

"You're dress. It's ruined," Phoebe says to Heather, she looks down and notices the blood.

"Evanescet," Lizzie murmurs. The stain disappears.

"Do you have a spell for everything?" Erik asks. Lizzie nods.

"Do you need to know who cursed him?" Phoebe asks Lizzie.

"No, I can undo the witches magic without needing her," Lizzie answers.

"I don't understand. You're the only witch we know about, the only one who knows the family. Why would a random witch curse this child?" Erik asks, Lizzie looks at him.

"I don't..." She starts before stopping.

"What's wrong?" Heather asks. Lizzie looks at the floor where Rafael is lying.

"It was the whole point. He knows another witch; he wanted it to look like I did it. He needed a reason to make you guys turn against me, what better way to do that then to make you believe I'm the reason your child and nephew is dead," Lizzie informs them. They all look at a sleeping Rafael. Elliot walks in followed by Nathan.

"What did I miss?" He asks. Lizzie ignores him and walks over to Rafael; she bends down and touches his head.

"Ostende nobis," she speaks. The room goes dark and Rafael's memories start flooding the room. It shows him talking to a young girl before handing her one of Henry's toys. She whispers something and the memory stops.

"What was that?" Nathan asks.

"It was Rafael, he's the reason Henry is cursed. He wanted to blame Lizzie," Phoebe informs them. Lizzie stands up, she walks over to the table where Elliot put the cup, knife and a bucket. She picks up the knife, everyone looks at her concerned. She notices.

"Relax, if I was going to kill him. I wouldn't use a knife," she says before walking over to Henry, she sits next to him. Henry is lying down.

"Hey Henry, I need to borrow some of your blood. I promise it won't hurt," she tells him.

"How do you know?" Henry asks weakly.

"Because your mum is going to take the pain away before you feel it," she replies. She turns and looks at Heather.

"I don't know how to do that," Heather responds.

"Don't worry. You'll pick it up," Lizzie informs her. Heather walks over to the table and perches on the edge, she picks up Henrys wrist and places over the bucket underneath him. Lizzie looks at her before cutting it. Henry winces and Heather squeezes his hand, and he starts to calm down.

"See, you're getting the hang of it," Lizzie says. She collects some of his blood in the bucket. His wrist heals and Lizzie gets up. She wipes the knife cleans and puts the bucket on the table, she holds out her hand to Heather. She hands it over and Lizzie cuts her too.

"What are you doing?" Erik asks.

"Collecting his blood and his parents. It will work as a counter spell. Stop the curse and save his life," Lizzie tells him. She lets go of Heathers wrist and looks at Elliot and holds the knife out to him. He walks over and cuts his hand; he holds it over the bucket.

"Expergisci," Lizzie says, Rafale wakes up. He stands up when he sees everyone.

"What did you do to me?" He asks.

"I put you to sleep, you were annoying me," Lizzie informs him. Elliot removes his hand and gives Lizzie the knife.

"Whatever," Rafael says, he turns.

"Rafael," Lizzie responds. He stops and turns to look at her. She walks towards him, grab his hand and cuts it. He groans in pain and pulls his hand back. She holds the bucket up.

"Don't be such a baby," she says to him. He holds his hand over the bucket while glaring at Lizzie. When she's finished, she walks back towards the table.

"Abolebitque," she says raising her hand at the bucket, it sets on fire. A few seconds later it's finished, and the flame goes. Lizzie picks up the bucket and tips the blood into the cup. She hands it to Henry.

"Drink up. This will make you all better," she tells him. He looks at his parents they nod, and he drinks it. The colour comes back to his face.

"It worked," Heather says relieved. She hugs her son.

"Of course, it worked. Lizzie is awesome," Erik tells them.

"Why did you need my blood?" Rafael asks.

"For fun. It amused me getting to cut you," Lizzie tells him. He lets out an irritated sigh and storms out the room. Lizzie looks at Elliot and Heather who are sitting with their son smiling. Phoebe and Nathan go over to them. Lizzie leaves. Heather gets up and follows.

"Lizzie, wait," she says. Lizzie stops and turns to look at her.

"Thank you, for what you just did and I'm sorry," Heather tells her.

"You don't need to apologise," Lizzie responds.

"I do. You have been so kind and understanding about this whole thing. You lost the person you loved, and you've handled it with grace and dignity. Not many people would be able to do that," Heather says. Lizzie looks at her.

"I won't lie, in the beginning I wasn't okay. I was actually trying to find ways to get rid of you. But seeing you guys together, seeing how happy you are, I realised I couldn't do that to him. He already lost someone he loved and that broke him, I couldn't be the reason he went through that again. You have a family together and you have a future. What sort of person would I be if I destroyed that?" Lizzie speaks. She walks away.

A week later Lizzie is sitting in The Joint with some textbooks. Heather walks in and goes over to her.

"Hey," Lizzie says looking up at her.

"Hey, can I sit?" Heather asks pointing at the empty seat.

"Sure," Lizzie responds. Heather sits down.

"What are you doing?" Heather asks.

"Work. Apparently, I'm failing most of my classes and if I don't catch up, I won't get to graduate," Lizzie replies.

"Wow, you're taking this whole school thing pretty seriously," Heather says.

"Wouldn't you?" Lizzie asks. Heather looks at her and picks up a thick book.

"There's so much to do," she says.

"The more lessons you're failing, the more work you have to do," Lizzie responds.

"Would you like some help?" Heather asks.

"No, I'm good for now. Thanks though," Lizzie answers. Taylor walks over and hands her a drink.

"Hey Lizzie, I got you that interview tomorrow," he tells her.

"Great, thank you," Lizzie responds.

"No worries," Taylor replies before walking away. Heather looks at her.

"Interview?" She asks.

"Yeah, I'm hoping to get a job," Lizzie answers.

"Good for you. You'll make a great waitress," Heather says. They sit there in silence for a minute.

"How's Henry?" Lizzie asks.

"Much better thanks to you," Heather replies.

"What about Rafael?" Lizzie asks.

"He doesn't know that we know," Heather answers. Lizzie's phone beeps.

"I have to go," she says standing up, she grabs her bag and books. "I'll see you around," she speaks before leaving. She heads outside where Erik and Phoebe are. Once they see her Erik grabs her books and Phoebe pulls her into an alleyway. Lizzie looks at them.

"What?" She asks.

"We have a problem," Phoebe tells her.

Chapter 7
Hunters

"What's the problem?" Lizzie asks.

"There are hunters in town," Erik responds.

"Hunters? As in vampire hunters?" Lizzie asks. Phoebe nods.

"How do you know this?" Lizzie questions them.

"We've seen them. They were unloading a van with a lot of gear. They headed into the woods," Phoebe informs her.

"What do we do?" Erik asks. Lizzie thinks for a minute.

"Nothing," she says.

"What?" Phoebe and Erik ask at the same time.

"We won't do anything. They won't do anything without proof that we're vampires, so we're just going to pretend that we don't know anything. We will go to school on Monday and act like normal teenagers. Don't give them a reason to suspect you," Lizzie tells them.

"What if they already know?" Erik asks.

"Then we'd already be dead," Lizzie replies.

Back at the Jones house Alex, Sam and Ben are sitting around on the sofas talking.

"How do you know our sister?" Alex asks.

"We met a few years ago," Ben answers.

"Have you always liked her?" Sam asks. Ben looks at him.

"Not at first," he replies.

"What about your family? Where are they?" Alex questions.

"Are they dead?" Sam queries. Vikki comes into the room.

"What is this, twenty-one questions. Leave him alone," Vikki tells them.

"We just want to make sure he's good enough," Alex tells her.

"Who's good enough?" Lizzie asks coming through the door.

"No one," Sam says. She looks at them all.

"How is your work coming along?" Vikki asks her.

"It's okay," Lizzie answers.

"Would you like some help?" Ben queries.

"Yes," Lizzie says. He gets up and they go upstairs.

"Door stay opens!" Alex shouts after them. Sam and Vikki chuckle.

The next day at school, a girl is in her locker. She's short with brown hair that goes just below her shoulders. She closes her locker; Lizzie is standing there.

"It's Leah, right?" She asks. Leah goes to turn the other way. Phoebe appears. She bares her teeth at her. Leah steps back.

"Let's talk," Lizzie declares. She turns around and walks off. Phoebe pushes Leah after her. They go into the girl's toilet; Phoebe locks the door.

"I didn't do anything. I don't even know who you are," Leah says.

"Well, we know who you are," Lizzie reminds her.

"What do you want?" Leah asks.

"How do you know Rafael?" Phoebe questions. Leah looks at her.

"Who?" She asks.

"Rafael Rodriguez, he got you to curse a child," Lizzie responds. Leah sighs and steps back to the sink.

"I don't. I don't even know how he found out about me. He just approached me one day. I didn't want to do it, but he threatened my family," Leah explains.

"That sounds like Rafael," Lizzie states.

"Am I in trouble?" Leah asks.

"Yes. That child you cursed was my nephew and he was going to die," Phoebe tells her.

"How do you guys know him?" Leah quizzes.

"He's, my brother," Phoebe says. Leah looks at her.

"So, he wanted me to curse his own child?" She asks puzzled. Lizzie laughs a little.

"No, it was his nephew too. They have a big family. Look we didn't come here to cause an issue, we just wanted to talk. Find out why you did it," Lizzie assures her.

"I told you," Leah says.

"I know," Lizzie replies.

"Did he die? The child?" Leah asks.

"No, Lizzie saved him," Phoebe answers. Leah looks at her.

"You're a witch too!" She says.

"Half-witch," Lizzie says.

"What's the other half?" Leah asks. Lizzie shows her teeth.

"Oh, cool," Leah says with uncertainty. She looks at Phoebe.

"I'm sorry for casting that curse. Truly. But if everything's fine now, what do you want me for?" She asks her.

"How long have you known that you're a witch?" Phoebe asks.

"A year. I'm still pretty new to it," Leah answers.

"That spell you cast. It was pretty hard. Even I don't know how to do that, and I've been a witch longer. How'd you learn?" Lizzie queries.

"I found it in one of my mum's books. I didn't know what it did," Leah says.

"Well, there's a lesson, don't use magic if you don't know what the outcome will be," Phoebe vocalises.

"Have you spoken to Rafael since that day?" Lizzie asks her.

"Yes, he has my number. He messages me when he wants a spell," Leah responds. Lizzie looks at Phoebe and then takes Leah's phone.

"I've given you, my number. Every time Rafael messages you, I want you to forward it to me. Can you do that?" Lizzie asks her. Leah nods and Lizzie hands her the phone. She leaves with Phoebe.

They're walking down the hallway when Jake approaches them.

"Hey guys. Can I ask you something?" He asks.

"You just did," Lizzie tells him. He looks at her and Phoebe chuckles.

"What's up?" Lizzie asks.

"Well tomorrow night is a full moon, and I can't seem to get rid of Mia. Can you guys help?" He questions.

"What do you want us to do? Lock her in a basement?" Phoebe asks. Jake looks at her horrified.

"No. Her friend, Mandy has told everyone that I'm throwing a party. All I need is for you guys to keep her distracted while I disappear for the night. Stop her from thinking about me," Jake replies.

"You know, I could just remove her memories of you for the night and then give them back in the morning," Lizzie informs him.

"You can do that?" Jake asks. Lizzie nods.

"Jake! There you are. I was starting to think you disappeared," Mia says going over with Mandy.

"No, I was just talking to my friends," Jake responds. Mia looks at the girls.

"I don't believe I've had the pleasure," she tells them.

"This is Phoebe. She's the one who's brother I was telling you about," Mandy reminds her.

"Oh, and you are?" Mia asks Lizzie.

"Elizabeth," Lizzie replies.

"Oh, you're Sam's twin," Mandy says.

"That would be me," Lizzie responds.

"Well, you guys should try out for the cheerleading team. I think you'd perfect," Mandy tells them.

"Aren't auditions over? It's nearly Christmas," Phoebe responds.

"Don't be silly. There's always room for new people," Mandy speaks before walking away. Mia and Jake follow.

"She seems like a piece of work," Lizzie says to Phoebe.

"Oh, she is," Phoebe replies.

That evening Lizzie and Taylor are at the joint.

"I'm so happy to finally be working with someone who's company I enjoy," Taylor says. Lizzie looks at him and smiles.

"I'm just happy to be working with someone I know," Lizzie replies. Taylor goes over to a table.

"Look at you, I didn't realise the uniform could actually look nice," Nathan says going over to Lizzie.

"What do you want?" Lizzie asks. Nathan smirks.

"For once love, I don't need anything off you," Nathan answers. Lizzie looks at him.

"Really?" She asks.

"Really. I just came because I'm hungry. That's all," Nathan replies before walking off. The door opens and a big muscly guy walks through with two smaller men. Lizzie walks over to them.

"Hi, is there anything I can help you with?" She asks.

"Do you work here?" The man questions.

"Yes," Lizzie replies.

"Great, I have a favour to ask." The man speaks, he pulls out a small bottle and hands it to her.

"Is there any chance you can put this is your drinks?" He asks her. Lizzie looks at him.

"Are you serious? You want me to spike people's drinks with some weird looking liquid and you're not going to tell me why or what it is?" Lizzie queries. The two smaller men chuckle.

"If I told you, you wouldn't believe me," The man responds.

"Try me," Lizzie says to him. Taylor walks over.

"I'm sorry, is something wrong?" He asks.

"Yes, where's your manager?" The man asks them.

"He's not here," Taylor informs him.

"We'll just come back when he is," The man says before turning and walking away followed by his men. Taylor looks at Lizzie and Nathan goes over.

"What is that?" Taylor asks.

"Vervain," Nathan replies taking the bottle from Lizzie's hand. Taylor looks at her.

"It's an herb that weakens vampires. Those men are hunters who arrived here yesterday," Lizzie tells him.

"When does your shift finish?" Nathan questions Lizzie.

"Nine, why?" She asks.

"Because I'm walking you back. Something tells me they know what you are. Your life could be in danger," Nathan informs her.

"I can handle myself," Lizzie reminds him.

"Oh, I know, but there's still strength in numbers," Nathan responds. Lizzie rolls her eyes and walks off.

"Who is the manager?" Nathan asks Taylor.

"My dad," Taylor replies.

The next day Lizzie throws on some leggings, a white top and Nathan's leather jacket. She ties her hair up and sneaks out the window. She heads towards the woods where Erik and Phoebe are waiting.

"What are we doing here again?" Erik asks.

"We're going hunting," Lizzie replies. She heads into the woods. Erik looks at Phoebe before following. They walk for a while, further into the woods.

"How will we even know when we're near, I mean they are hunters after all. They'll have the jump on us," Erik says. Lizzie holds up her hand and Erik goes silent. He can't speak.

"We're here," Lizzie tells her.

"Okay, but was that necessary?" Phoebe asks pointing at Erik.

"Yes, see those trees they have speakers all around them, set up to report back any unauthorised voices to the main source. That source will be on the campsite. They would only set the speakers up around the camp so no one could get to close. Anyone talking past this area is dead. We have to go the rest of the way in silence," Lizzie informs them.

"How do you know that?" Phoebe asks.

"Because there not very smart. If you listen, you can hear the speaker letting out small vibrations. Since the vibrations don't come as far as here, it must mean that this is the safe zone," Lizzie replies. Phoebe just looks at Erik.

"If you can manage not speaking, I'll give you your voice back," Lizzie tells him. Erik nods. Lizzie waves her hand, and his voice comes back.

"Do exactly as I do. Don't make any sudden movements. We don't know how many people are on the campsite," Lizzie warns them before walking off. They follow. They sneak towards the camp and hide in one of the bushes. They look onto the camp. The two skinny guys from yesterday are standing on the far side.

"There's another guy in the tent. I can hear him talking on the radio," Phoebe whispers. Lizzie looks at her before lifting her hand up. She focuses on the tent. The guy in the tent screams and comes out. The two guys run towards him.

"Hunter, what's wrong?" One of them asks.

"The radio sparked up in my hand. It electrocuted me and then stopped working," he replies.

"I'll check the tower," The other guy says and walks off. Lizzie looks at Erik.

"Follow him. Then go home. We'll be there after you," she whispers. Erik nods and leaves. Once he's gone out of sight, she looks at Phoebe.

"You ready?" She asks. Phoebe nods. They jump out the bushes and Phoebe takes down the guard. Hunter runs into the tent.

"It's Hunter, right? If you come out now, we won't kill your friend," Lizzie says. Phoebe grins at her. Hunter comes out.

"Funny you should say that I was thinking the same thing," he replies. The guy on the floor twists Phoebe round and injects her. Phoebe screams. Lizzie goes to run over to her, but Hunter appears in front of her.

"I wouldn't," he tells her. The guy pulls Phoebe up off the floor and blows a whistle. The other guard comes rushing back a few minutes later.

"What's going on?" He asks.

"Help me; even with vervain she's still strong," The other guard tells him. He goes over and helps hold Phoebe.

"My friends could kill her," he tells Lizzie.

"I highly doubt it," Lizzie replies. She goes to hold her hand up when Hunter drops something in front of her. It makes a small explosion and sends Lizzie to the ground.

"It's a new invention our boss made. It has the right ingredients to kill a vampire within a few seconds of breathing in the fumes," Hunter tells her.

"Why are you doing this?" Lizzie asks.

"I have to. I'm following orders. You guys are a danger. You kill or feed on innocent people to survive," Hunter replies.

"I've never done that," Lizzie says.

"Liar, if you never fed of anyone, you would off died a long time ago," Hunter replies.

"No, I wouldn't have. I just eat normal food," Lizzie tells him. He looks at her. Just then three other men arrive.

"What do we have here?" One asks.

"Vampires, they invaded the camp. Hunter used the device on her," One of the guys explains.

"Then why isn't she dead?" Another one asks. They all look at her.

"What are you?" Hunter asks. Lizzie goes to reply when she starts coughing up blood. Phoebe struggles in the guy's arms.

"You have to help her," she says.

"Help her? Why would we?" One of the guards asks. Hunter holds his hand up.

"What's your name?" He asks her.

"Phoebe," she replies.

"And what about your friend," Hunter asks looking at Lizzie on the floor.

"Elizabeth," Phoebe replies.

"Tell me Phoebe, what are you guys? If you were vampires, she would be dead. And you would be heavily sedated with the amount of vervain in your system," Hunter asks.

"I'm a hybrid and Lizzie; she's a vampire and a witch. She's from the eclipse coven," Phoebe answers. Hunter looks surprised for a minute before looking at Lizzie and panicking.

"The cure," he says. He turns towards the tent and goes to run into it.

"What do you think you're doing?" One of the guys asks.

"I'm saving her life," Hunter replies.

"I don't think so," he says pulling out a remote. He presses the red button and Hunter falls to the floor.

"Don't forget, we control you," The guard says.

Erik arrives home. He walks through the door and sees Rafael and Leah.

"What's she doing here?" Erik asks.

"Helping me with something. Where are the girls?" Rafael questions.

"They should be behind me," Erik answers.

"Where did you guys go?" Rafael asks irritated.

"Into the woods, after the hunters," he says. Rafael looks at him.

"Tell me everything," He demands.

Hunter gets off the floor.

"Stop!" He says to them.

"You don't tell us what to do," The guy replies.

"She needs help," Hunter responds.

"No, she's a vampire. We are here to kill all vampires," The guy replies. Lizzie stops moving and lies still.

"No!" Phoebe screams. All of a sudden, the main guard goes flying. Rafael and Leah arrive. Phoebe breaks free and kills the two guys holding her. Rafael kills the other two and then grabs the guard off the floor. Leah looks at Hunter.

"No, he's their prisoner. The bracelet," Phoebe tells her. Leah looks at it and casts a spell, the bracelet falls off. Hunter sighs in relief.

"Finally," he says feeling his wrist. Phoebe looks at him.

"You said you'd help her," she reminds him. He goes into the tent and comes out with a bottle.

"I need your blood; the vampire side will help it work faster," he tells her holding up a knife. Phoebe lifts her hand.

"No," Rafael says. Phoebe looks at him. "It could be a trick," he tells her.

"It's not. I only want to help," Hunter replies. Rafael looks between him, Phoebe and an unconscious Lizzie on the floor.

"Then use mine," he says looking at Leah. Leah nods and pins the guy to the tree with her magic. He walks towards them and holds his hand out; Hunter cuts it with the knife and adds the blood to the bottle. He shakes it, adds it to a needle then injects Lizzie. He mutters a spell when he's finished and touches her head.

"What did you do?" Rafael asks.

"It's a healing spell, it should help," Hunter replies. Rafael walks towards the guy.

"Where are the rest of you?" He asks. The guy just smiles.

"I'm telling you nothing," he replies.

"Fine, have it your way," Rafael responds. He rips his heart out.

"Let's move. They could be back at any time," Rafael tells them. He walks over and picks Lizzie up.

"You're coming with us until she's better and if anything, bad happens to her. I'll kill you myself," Rafael warns him before walking off. Phoebe looks at him sympathetically before following with Leah. Hunter sighs.

"Great, I get free just to become someone else's prisoner," he says before walking off.

They walk through Lizzie's front door. Alex rushes over.

"What did you do?" Alex asks Rafael.

"He didn't do anything, he saved her," Leah replies.

"It's true," Phoebe tells them as she walks through the door with Hunter. Sam recognises him and flies across the room. He grabs Hunter by the neck and slams him against the wall.

"I know you. This was you're doing," he says angrily. Phoebe goes over.

"Let him go. He was only helping," Phoebe tells him.

"Yeah right," Sam replies.

"It wasn't his fault; he was their prisoner. They were controlling him. He's here to help her. Now let him go," Phoebe responds showing her teeth. Sam looks at her and does the same.

"Sam," Alex says taking Lizzie off Rafael. Sam puts his teeth away and lets him go. He looks at Alex.

"That's enough!" He warns him. Sam sighs.

"Thank you, Rafael," Alex says before heading upstairs with Lizzie. Sam looks at Hunter before following. A few minutes later they come back downstairs.

"She's resting," Alex tells them.

"We leave you guys alone. I'll come by tomorrow," Phoebe says walking towards the front door with Leah and Rafael. Hunter goes to follow.

"I don't think so," Sam says stepping in front of him. Hunter stops.

"If you're here to help my sister, you will be staying under this roof where I can keep an eye on you," Sam tells him.

"That isn't necessary. I'll help her anyway," Hunter responds.

"Guest room is first door on your right," Sam says pointing towards the stairs. Hunter sighs and goes up the stairs. A few minutes later, Ben walks in.

"Hey, I've just seen Taylor. He says Lizzie didn't show up for her shift. Have you seen her?" He asks them.

"She's upstairs," Alex responds. Ben heads up the stairs and walks into Lizzie's room. Hunter is sitting on her bed muttering a spell. Ben hisses and chucks him across the room. Hunter stands up and looks at him.

"Who are you?" Ben asks with his teeth showing.

"I'm the help," Hunter responds. Ben looks at Lizzie who is pale.

"I don't believe you," he replies. Hunter growls at him and his eyes turn green, his teeth show. They both snarl and run at each other. Hunter chucks Ben into the draws. Ben gets angry and charges at Hunter. They collide onto the floor. Alex and Sam rush in.

"Enough!" Alex shouts. The boys stop and get up.

"What is going on?" He asks them.

"Ask this lunatic," Hunter answers.

"You're the one putting a spell on Lizzie," Ben says.

"Maybe we should introduce you guys. Hunter, meet Ben, Lizzie's friend. Ben, meet Hunter, Lizzie's doctor," Alex introduces them.

"Why does she need a doctor?" Ben asks.

"I don't," Lizzie answers getting up. She looks around her room and sees it destroyed.

"Do I even want to know?" She asks. They all shake their heads.

"Can somebody please explain what's going on?" Ben asks.

"I'd like to know that too. You were prepared to kill me in the woods until you found out what I was, what changed?" Lizzie asks Hunter.

"You're from the eclipse coven. It's very rare to find anyone part of that coven, they're pretty much extinct. When

I found out you were from there, I had to save you," Hunter explains.

"Why?" Lizzie asks.

"I'm part of that coven too," Hunter answers.

"You're a witch?" Sam asks.

"And werewolf," Hunter responds.

"What happened to the coven?" Lizzie asks.

"They were one of the strongest, people seen them as a threat. Sometimes they took their powers too far. It caused problems for other supernatural's. In the end, they called in a professional group called the Venandi. The coven got wiped out," Hunter briefs them.

"I'm sorry, go back. Who or what is a Venandi?" Sam asks.

"It's Latin for hunter," Lizzie answers. She looks at Hunter.

"The men you came here with, that's who they are right?" She questions.

"Yes. I was the only survivor from the coven. They kept me as prisoner to help them. They needed my magic to seek out other supernatural creatures. It led us to this town. The supernatural radar was extremely high," Hunter explains.

"There's not that many here. Only like thirteen," Alex speaks.

"That you know off. The radar shows everything. Not only who is but also who could be. Werewolves and witches that don't know they're supernatural yet," Hunter explains.

"Do you know who they are?" Sam asks.

"Not their names. It just gives us a number," Hunter responds. Lizzie looks at him.

"How many people did you get?" She asks.

"Twenty," Hunter answers. Everyone looks at each other.

"We need to find the missing seven before they do," Lizzie tells her brothers. Just then Vikki walks into the bedroom.

"Lizzie, you have a visitor," Vikki tells her. Taylor walks in.

"Lizzie, I need your help," he says.

Chapter 8
New Wolf

Lizzie looks at Taylor, his hands are shaking, and he has become really sweaty.

"Taylor, what happened?" Lizzie asks.

"It was an accident. He came out of nowhere. I think he's dead," Taylor tries to explain.

"Wait, you killed somebody?" Alex asks.

"Hit them with my car," Taylor answers. His leg cracks and he falls to the floor in agony.

"I don't know what's wrong," he tells Lizzie. She looks out the window and sees the moon rising. She looks at her brothers.

"It's a full moon," she says before looking at Taylor. More of his bones break.

"Taylor you're a werewolf," she announces.

"What? How?" Taylor questions.

"It's a curse. You're forced to turn on the full moon once you've triggered it," Hunter informs him.

"How do you trigger it?" Taylor asks.

"You kill somebody," Lizzie answers. Taylor's ankle breaks and he screams. Alex, Sam, Ben and Vikki step back.

"Help me!" Taylor cries out. Lizzie looks at Hunter.

"You have to take him outside. He can't change in here," Lizzie informs him. Hunter goes over to Taylor and puts his arm over his shoulder, he heads out the room. Lizzie pulls out her phone.

"Call Elliot," she tells Alex before leaving.

"Where are you going?" Ben asks.

"To call Phoebe, we're supposed to be at a party," Lizzie responds before leaving. She heads outside and sees Taylor lying on the lawn at the far end. Hunter is standing close to him.

"I don't know what to do," he says going over to Lizzie.

"It's fine. Help should be here shortly," Lizzie informs him. She dials a number on her phone and holds it to her ear. After a while, she puts it down.

"No answer," she says.

"You may have a bigger problem," Hunter tells her. She follows his gaze across the lawn where it's gone quiet. There's just a shape lying there.

"Taylor?" Lizzie vocalises slowly walking towards him. The shape gets up and stands on all fours as a wolf. Hunter grabs Lizzie's arm.

"Run," he says quietly. The wolf emerges from the dark growling at Lizzie and Hunter.

"Lizzie run!" Hunter shouts. Lizzie turns to run when a shape jumps over her and stands between her and the wolf. Lizzie notices it's Rafael he growls loudly at the Taylor who is now a wolf. Taylor turns and runs. Rafael stands straight, he turns to look at Lizzie and Hunter with red eyes.

"I'd never thought I'd say this, but I'm glad to see you," Lizzie tells him. Rafael smiles and his eyes go back to normal.

"You're an alpha?" Hunter asks.

"Yep, the only one in town," Rafael replies.

"What's going to happen to Taylor?" Lizzie asks him.

"Don't worry. Elliot and Nathan are in the woods. They'll lead him somewhere safe," Rafale informs her. Lizzie nods. Rafael stands there for a minute, him and Lizzie avoiding eye contact.

"Well, I should probably get going," Rafael says. He walks away.

"That was awkward, ex-lovers?" Hunter questions.

"Ew, no. Never," Lizzie tells him. They head inside.

"What happened? Are you okay?" Alex asks Lizzie.

"I'm fine. Rafael showed up," Lizzie replies. She looks at Hunter.

"I know that an Alpha has red eyes and that a new werewolf has golden. But Taylor's were blue, why?" Lizzie asks.

"If you're from a family of royalty, then your eyes turn blue. It shows other people that you're important," Hunter responds.

"So, then Rafael isn't the only alpha in town?" Lizzie asks. Hunter shakes his head.

"Taylor's dad or mum would have to be one for him to have blue eyes," Hunter responds.

"What about green eyes?" Ben asks.

"Green? I don't think that's a thing," Lizzie says.

"It is. He has them," Ben points out. Everyone looks at Hunter and he sighs.

"My eyes aren't to do with being a wolf, it's to do with my witch side. If a witches eyes turn green, it means that they've been condemned by anger and hatred. It means they've killed someone and can't control their dark side. If not taught how to control it, an evil spirit will take over them. Most witches are known to be lost once that happens," Hunter explains.

"So how many people have you killed?" Ben questions.

"Three and I regret them all, but it doesn't matter how I feel. My eyes are damaged forever," Hunter responds, his eyes flash green.

"I think your eyes are pretty cool. Damaged or not." Lizzie assures him. He smiles at her gratefully. Ben looks at him, eyes full of rage. Lizzie notices.

"I still need some help with my schoolwork. Ben, would you like to help?" Lizzie asks. She walks towards the stairs. "Ben?" She says sternly. Ben tears his eyes away from Hunter.

"I'm coming," he tells her and follows her up the stairs. They head into Lizzie's room and Ben closes the door behind them.

"Look Ben," Lizzie starts, she turns around and Ben kisses her.

"What happened to waiting?" Lizzie asks.

"I don't want to wait anymore," Ben tells her. Lizzie takes his hands.

"Look Ben, we can't be together right now. There's too much going on. You need to wait or move on," Lizzie tells him. He looks at her before leaving the room.

The next day at school, Jake is in his locker, Lizzie goes over to him.

"Jake, what colour are your eyes?" She asks. Jake looks in the mirror.

"Brown," He replies. Lizzie smiles.

"No, I can see that. I mean your werewolf eyes," She responds. Jake looks at her and closes his locker.

"Golden," He tells her before walking off. She follows him.

"Who does Taylor live with?" She queries. Jake stops and looks at her.

"His dad. When he was five, his mum died, never had any siblings. Why?" Jake asks.

"Because Taylor's eyes are blue," Lizzie informs him. Jake looks at her confused for a minute before pulling her into a nearby classroom.

"Taylor is a werewolf?" He asks. She nods.

"Found out last night when he accidentally killed someone. Oh wait, how did you trigger it?" Lizzie asks.

"I have anger issues. Three years ago, I was riding my bike home from school when some lad tried to start a fight, I pushed him over and he split his head open. I never told anyone because I wasn't proud of it. Even to this day I'm still ashamed," Jake explains.

"I get it. We all have things in our past we want to change, it can't define us though. We have to learn to let the pass go or we'll never have a positive future," Lizzie assures him. Jake looks at her.

"What were you saying about Taylor?" He asks.

"Right, his eyes were blue. We think his dad might be the alpha of a pack. We just don't know which one," Lizzie responds.

"It's not my pack. I didn't even know his dad's a wolf, let alone the alpha," Jake says.

"Which pack do you come from?" Lizzie asks.

"Moonshine," Jake replies.

"How many packs are there?" She questions.

"Three. Moonshine, Shadow and Twilight," Jake informs her.

"It's not the shadow pack. Phoebe is in that one and her older brother is the alpha," Lizzie says.

"Then it has to be Twilight, they're the strongest pack. Mine is pretty much extinct," Jake speaks.

"Do you ever have meetings?" Lizzie questions.

"Yeah, we do pack meeting once a month before the full moon and twice a year they have this group meeting with the other packs, but it's normally the Alpha's and Betas that go to it," Jake informs her.

"Beta meaning Taylor. Who's your Alpha and Beta?" Lizzie asks.

"Our Alpha is a man called Tyron Watson. All we know is he has a son and is dangerous. He doesn't live in the town and we've never met the Beta," Jake announces. The bell goes.

"I have to get to lesson. We'll speak later," Jake says, he leaves the classroom.

Later that day Lizzie is sitting in the library looking through textbooks. Erik walks over and sits opposite her.

"What you doing?" He asks.

"I'm trying to find information," Lizzie responds.

"Information on what?" Erik queries.

"Werewolves. The full moon. The curse. More about Alpha's. anything really," Lizzie responds.

"And you think you'll find it in the school library?" Erik asks.

"Where else would I find it?" Lizzie questions.

"I don't know. It's just this is a school, why would they have books about supernatural creatures?" Erik queries.

"You'd be surprised. Everyone here believes it to be a myth not real. They'd have books here for educational purposes," Lizzie answers. Evie walks over with Brooke.

"Hey guys," Erik says.

"Hey, you don't mind if we sit?" Brooke asks sitting down anyway. Evie sits next to Erik.

"So, what you doing?" Brooke questions looking at the books stacked on the table.

"History. We're learning about supernatural's," Lizzie answers.

"You're so lucky. I've been begging my teacher to let us do that ever since I came across that book," Brooke announces. Erik and Lizzie look at her.

"What book?" Lizzie asks. Brooke opens her bag and pulls out a thick book. She hands it to Lizzie. Lizzie opens it and reads the first word.

"Watson Venandi," she says. Brooke looks at her.

"You know what that means?" She asks.

"It's Latin for 'supernatural'," Lizzie explains.

"Right, and how do you know Latin?" Brooke queries. Erik looks at Lizzie.

"I used to take it at my old school. French was boring," Lizzie responds.

"Cool, most of the book is in Latin then. There are some English words but not many. It still caught my attention though," Brooke replies. Lizzie looks at Erik and then Brooke.

"Can I borrow this for a while? I'll give it back," Lizzie tells her.

"Sure. If it will help you with your lesson," Brooke says. Just then the bell goes.

"Erik, we have a history lesson to get to," Lizzie says standing up. Erik looks at her confused, she pulls a face at him.

"Oh, right. We'll see you guys later," Erik declares standing up. Him and Lizzie leave.

They head down the hall, Lizzie walks towards the front door.

"Where are you going?" Erik asks her.

"Home. I lied in there. It's not a title on the front of the book. It's a name and I know whose name," Lizzie responds. Erik looks at her confused. Lizzie turns around and leaves.

"I'm going to get in so much trouble," Erik says to himself before leaving.

Lizzie walks through her front door. Alex, Ben and Sam all look at her. Hunter is sitting on the sofas; she walks over and chucks the book in front of him.

"That's your name on the front of the book. Why?" Lizzie asks. Hunter picks it up and looks at it.

"I don't know," he tells her. She looks at him.

"You think I'm going to believe that? You're a Watson. Your dad is the alpha of the moonshine pack and from what I hear, he's dangerous. You arrive in town and then a book appears with your name on it. You need to do a lot better than I don't know," Lizzie demands. Erik looks at her brothers and shrugs. Hunter gets up and walks towards her.

"I don't know what to tell you. Yes, my dad is an alpha and yes, he is dangerous. But he sold me to those Hunters once he found out I was part witch. He got my entire coven wiped off this earth and then killed my mother in front of me for being a witch. I don't know why this book has my name on it, I didn't even know it existed until now," Hunter announces.

"I don't believe you," Lizzie says. Hunter takes a closer step towards her.

"Of course, you don't. Why would you? After all your family is the one refusing to let me leave, I'm being held here against my own free will. You and your family are crazy and completely messed up. Do you know what it feels like to be held in a place you don't want to be, where you get forced to do things that you're not comfortable with. I hated the past two years of my life; they turned me into something I'm not."

"But you wouldn't know anything because you have a family that love you through everything, a family that supports you and celebrate your differences. They don't care that you're a witch because they're just happy to have you in their lives again. I'm never going to get the chance to reunite with my family. You don't have to believe me or trust me, but one thing is for sure, when my father comes to town, and he will. You're going to need all the friends you can get," Hunter warns her before going up the stairs.

"We really need to work on your people skills," Erik says to Lizzie. Everyone just looks at him.

Lizzie spends the afternoon reading the book, trying to figure out what it all means. At about seven, she gives up and leaves.

"Where are you going?" Sam shouts after her but she just ignores him. Hunter comes down the stairs, he goes over to the book.

"What are you doing?" Ben asks him.

"Helping, not because I care about any of you. But because I want to stop my dad and I can't do that if I don't know what's going on," Hunter answers.

"Maybe we don't need your help," Ben says.

"If that was true, you would have the answer already," Hunter tells him before leaving the room with the book.

"I really can't stand that guy," Ben speaks.

"Join the club," Sam replies. He holds up a drink, Ben goes over and joins him.

"Why don't you like him?" Ben asks.

"Two years ago, I was in New York following a lead about Lizzie. I stopped for a snack in an alleyway, Hunter caught me and captured me. Him and his friends held me hostage for three months before I escaped," Sam explains. Ben looks at him.

"Sounds like you need to return the favour," He responds.

"Why do you think he's not going anywhere?" Sam queries. Ben smiles at him.

After a while, Lizzie returns back and goes upstairs. She enters her room and finds Hunter standing there. She stops when she sees him.

"I know what the book means," Hunter tells her.

"I knew it," Lizzie responds.

"I didn't before, but after you left, I had a look. When I opened, it showed me something, something that we need to stop my dad from getting what he wants," Hunter informs her. Lizzie looks at him.

"What does he want?" She asks.

"I think you should call your friends over. They all need to hear this," Hunter says before leaving the room.

Once everyone has arrived Hunter enters the room. He goes up to the window area where Lizzie is.

"What's going on?" Phoebe asks.

"That's a good question, Hunter?" Lizzie responds.

"Yes. All of our lives are in danger," Hunter tells them. Everyone looks around the room.

"I'm sorry, what?" Jake asks.

"My father is coming to town and he's not a very nice man. After he found out that my mother was a witch, he became vengeful. He believes that all witches and vampires are a problem to this world, and he will destroy them all. He's also the alpha of the moonshine pack and he doesn't play well with other alphas and their packs. He'll kill them all too," Hunter explains.

"How do you know which pack you're in?" Taylor asks.

"Most people are born into one. As we discovered yesterday you are from the twilight pack and your dad is the alpha," Hunter answers. Taylor looks at him.

"Yeah, I'm still new to this whole thing. I have no idea what you're talking about," Taylor informs him. Lizzie chuckles and then walks to the bookshelf. She pulls out a book.

"Catch," she says throwing it at Taylor. He catches it.

"What is it?" He asks her.

"It's a book all about werewolf. Different packs, eye colours. What everything means. Read it and it will help you understand," Lizzie explains. Taylor sits down on the sofa.

"If you had that book here the whole time, why were you looking for more at school?" Erik asks her.

"That one's basic. Mainly for beginners. It didn't have what I was looking for," Lizzie answers.

"What do you mean by danger?" Nathan asks. Lizzie looks at Hunter.

"What? It doesn't get any easier to understand then that," Hunter tells her.

"We need the details. How long we have? How to stop him? The important bits," Heather says.

"Oh, right. Well, he will be here in about two weeks with an army and his only goal is to wipe out supernatural existence. And as for stopping him there's only one way," Hunter explains.

"Why do I feel like there's a but?" Elliot asks.

"Because there is. In order to stop him, we have to work together. As a team, without problems. Now I don't like most of you and I know that some of you don't like me either and once we've done this, I'm leaving," Hunter responds.

"You won't be missed," Ben informs him. Hunter smiles at him sarcastically.

"You'll be the one person I'd be glad to see the back off," Hunter speaks.

"Seriously guys? That's enough," Lizzie says stepping forward. She looks at everyone else.

"There's a weapon, we can use it. We just have to find it first," Lizzie tells them.

"Where can we find it?" Heather asks.

"We don't know yet. We're looking, but until then prepare yourselves for the worse," Lizzie says.

"Yes, because in two weeks, we're going to war," Hunter declares.

Chapter 9
The Invitation

The next day a letter arrives in the mail. Elliot takes it and joins his family in the living room.

"We have a letter," he says holding it up.

"It looks fancy," Phoebe says. Elliot opens it.

"It's an invitation," he tells them.

"What is it for?" Rafael asks not looking up from his newspaper. Elliot looks at them all before reading.

"This year the town will host a Christmas ball to celebrate its 50th year. Everybody will be expected to attend. A male and female from each household (if possible) will represent the town by arriving in style, with a date to start the part of with a dance. From the Rodriguez household, we have Phoebe and Rafael. We look forward to seeing you all on Friday for rehearsal," he finishes reading.

"Me? Why couldn't they have picked somebody else," Rafael groans. They just ignore him.

"It says we look forward to seeing you all, who else is on there," Nathan asks.

"Alexander and Elizabeth, they're representing their house," Elliot replies. Rafael groans.

"Great!" He says sarcastically before walking out. They all look at each other.

Alexander is reading the invitation out at his house.

"At least, I don't have to go," Sam says kicking back and relaxing.

"But you do," Lizzie replies. He looks at her.

"I'm guessing Evie will need a date, she could ask you," Lizzie tells him.

"She might not. Is she on there?" Sam asks.

"Yes, her and her brother from their household. Same as Taylor, Jake and Leah are all on there," Alex responds. Lizzie takes the invitation.

"There are quite a few on it," she says.

"You do realise tomorrow is Friday right, who will you attend with? We all know Alex will take Vikki but what about you? You could ask Ben but at the same time you've recently broke his heart, he probably hates you now. Or maybe you could ask Hunter but then again, he hates you too. Taylor's already going to be there and so is Jake. Do you have any other friends left?" Sam asks her. Lizzie throws a pillow at him and leaves the room.

"Something I said?" Sam queries. Vikki follows Lizzie. She heads into her room.

"Are you okay?" Vikki asks. Lizzie opens her draw.

"Yeah, do you really think Ben hates me?" She asks Vikki.

"No, I don't think Ben could ever hate you. I see the way he looks at you, it's full of love and admiration. Never hate," Vikki replies. Lizzie keeps looking through her draw.

"What are you looking for?" Vikki asks.

"My money, it's not here though," Lizzie responds.

"Why is it so important?" Vikki queries.

"Phoebe wants to go shopping for dresses," Lizzie replies.

"Just ask your brother for money," Vikki tells her.

"No, I'd never hear the end of it," Lizzie says. Vikki looks at her.

"It's fine honestly. I need to go anyway," Lizzie says before leaving. Just as she's leaving, Ben walks in. They look at each other for a minute before going their separate ways.

"Well, that was awkward," Sam states.

"Shut up," Vikki says to him.

Lizzie arrives in town and sees Phoebe and Nathan.

"What's he doing here?" Lizzie asks.

"Charming as always," Nathan responds.

"Nathan wanted to come shopping too," Phoebe says.

"More like I didn't have a choice," Nathan tells her. Lizzie smiles.

"Let's get this over with, shall we?" Nathan asks. They head into a shop; Phoebe goes over to a clothes rack and Nathan goes and sits on the sofa. Lizzie joins him.

"Not joining Phoebe?" He asks.

"Not in the mood," Lizzie answers.

"I got you something," he tells her. She looks up at him.

"You? Got me something?" Lizzie says sounding surprised.

"Don't sound so surprised love. You know you've always been my favourite. Besides, you've done me a few favours recently, even if it's caused you pain. I think a thank you is in order," Nathan informs her. He pulls out a small box from his jacket pocket and hands it to her. She reluctantly takes it.

"What is it?" She asks.

"Open it and find out," Nathan responds. She opens the box, inside is a silver sterling locket. She looks at Nathan.

"Thank you," Lizzie replies. Nathan smiles at her before taking it and taking it on.

"So, why aren't you in the mood for dress shopping?" He asks.

"I have nobody to go with," Lizzie answers.

"What about Ben?" Nathan asks.

"He isn't talking to me," Lizzie responds.

"Well," Nathan starts. Phoebe walks over.

"Lizzie, look," she says pointing across the shop. Lizzie looks over and sees Jake and Mia.

"You're breaking up with me?" Mia asks.

"Yes. Look Mia, I am sorry. But I can't be with you anymore, I've fallen for someone else," Jake explains.

"It was your party, wasn't it? You disappeared all night with this other girl," Mia says.

"Yes, I'm sorry," Jake responds before walking away.

"Who am I supposed to go to the ball with now?" Mia shouts after him as she stomps her foot on the ground.

"Who is that?" Nathan asks.

"Mia something. She's in school with us," Phoebe tells him.

"She is very pretty and as it would appear in need of a date. Excuse me a minute," he says getting up, he hands Phoebe a wad of money and walks away. Lizzie and Phoebe chuckle.

"He has got a thing for blondes," Phoebe speaks. Lizzie looks at her.

"Have you found a dress?" She asks her.

"No, not yet," Phoebe responds. She looks at Lizzie.

"Come on, let's find you the perfect dress. Something that says bouncing back from a heartbreak," Phoebe demands. She pulls her up and further into the shop. After what feels like forever, Phoebe steps out of the changing room and goes over to where Nathan is sitting with Mia.

"So, what do you think?" She asks.

"The same thing that is said about the last twelve. You look great," Nathan tells her without even looking up.

"What about Lizzie?" Phoebe asks pulling her out of the dressing room.

"What about her? She looks…" Nathan starts, he looks up and sees Lizzie standing there in a dress.

"Wow, Lizzie, you look. I mean, that dress is. I mean, you look amazing," Nathan sputters. Lizzie smiles.

"Thank you," she says. Nathan stares at her for a minute before tearing his eyes away.

"Right, well, if that's it, go and pay. I will be waiting outside," he tells them leaving quickly. Phoebe looks at Lizzie.

"I think you made somebody speechless," she says before heading into the changing room. Lizzie follows. They arrive outside the shop.

"Finally, I was starting to think you changed your mind again," Nathan declares.

"No, we were just talking," Phoebe tells him.

"Right. We should be heading back. Lizzie, we'll walk you first," Nathan says.

Back at the Jones, Alex and Vikki are in his bedroom.

"I'm just saying, as her older brother you should help her out. Find someone to go with her," Vikki pleads. Alex sighs and Hunter walks past the room.

"Hey, wolf boy," Alex shouts. Hunter stops and walks back towards the door.

"Yes?" He asks with attitude.

"Drop the attitude. I have a favour to ask," Alex tells him.

"What is it?" Hunter asks.

"I need you to offer to accompany my sister to this Christmas ball thing next week," Alex informs him.

"And why would I do that?" Hunter asks.

"Because I'm asking nicely," Alex replies.

"More like demanding. Why don't you just get the other one to do it. It's easy to tell he likes her. Besides, I don't have to do what you tell me," Hunter points out before walking away. Alex gets up and leaves the room, he heads into the room Ben is in. He's sitting on his bed; he looks up when Alex comes in.

"Hey, what's up?" Ben asks.

"You like my sister, right?" Alex asks.

"Yes, but she doesn't want to be together," Ben answers.

"But you like her enough to help her out?" Alex questions. Ben nods.

"Great, will you accompany her to the ball next week?" Alex says.

"Sure," Ben responds.

"That was easy," Alex replies. Ben looks at him.

"I'd do anything for Lizzie, that will never change," Ben informs him.

"That's good to know," Alex says before leaving.

Lizzie arrives back and goes to her room. She hangs her dress up and her door knocks.

"Come in," she shouts. The door opens, and Ben comes in.

"Ben," she says with a surprised tone.

"Hey, I came to ask you something," Ben tells her.

"Okay, what is it?" Lizzie asks.

"Would you like to go to the ball with me?" Ben asks. Lizzie looks at him for a minute.

"Sure, I would like that," she tells him. Hunter appears behind Ben.

"As much as I despise the pair of you, there's something you need to know," he says. Ben rolls his eyes and then turns around.

"What? What could possibly be so important. After all, your life is boring," Ben points out.

"It's about my father. He will be arriving the day before the ball," Hunter informs them.

"Why?" Lizzie asks.

"My guess is it will be easier for him to catch all supernatural's. Everyone will be there," Hunter says.

"Okay, so he'll be arriving on Thursday. That still gives us time," Lizzie replies.

"Yes, it does. If you can stop gazing at each other for long enough to actually help," Hunter responds before turning and walking away. Lizzie looks at Ben apologetically and then follows. She goes downstairs and over to her workspace.

"You don't have to be so rude you know," she says to Hunter.

"Perhaps, but then again it's not like any of you are my friends," Hunter reminds her.

"I would be your friend, you're the one with the issues," Lizzie points out. Hunter looks at her.

"You'd really be my friend?" He asks.

"Of course, like you said. You saved my life because were from the same coven, we don't need to be enemies," Lizzie answers. Hunter smiles to himself before helping with the spell. A few hours later Hunter is slouched across the bay window dozing off, Lizzie is standing next to the table muttering a few words. The dish she's working on goes up in flames. She jumps back and Hunter darts up. He stands and goes over to her. The flame dies down.

"What happened?" He asks. Lizzie looks at him before walking towards the table. She leans over the dish and picks up a silver knife. She holds it up to him.

"You are amazing," Hunter tells her.

"Tell me something I don't know," Lizzie says. He grins and takes it off her.

"I didn't think we'd actually be able to do it," Hunter speaks.

"What can I say? I'm very determined, I don't give up easily," she warns him.

"What's going on in here?" Sam asks entering the room with the rest.

"We made a silver knife, designed to kill an alpha," Lizzie informs them.

"Seriously? Let me see that," Alex demands going over and taking it. He studies it for a minute before looking at them both.

"Well done. I didn't think you could do it," he says handing it back to Lizzie and walking away.

The next day Lizzie and Ben head to the town hall for rehearsals. Most of the other people are there already. Lizzie notices Nathan, he walks towards her.

"I didn't think you'd be here," Lizzie says to him.

"I can be pretty persuasive if I need to," Nathan responds.

"Where's your sister?" Lizzie asks.

"Not here yet. Although when she gets here, I fear it might cause a problem," Nathan tells her.

"Why?" Lizzie questions.

"It would appear that the girl Jake dumped Mia for, is my sister," Nathan informs her.

"Yikes. Poor Mia," Lizzie says.

"Hey, have you signed in yet?" Mia asks going over.

"That's a thing?" Lizzie asks. Mia smiles.

"Come on, I'll take you," Mia responds pulling Lizzie away. Ben goes to follow, and Nathan grabs his arm. Ben looks at him.

"If you hurt her, I will kill you," Nathan warns him. Ben pulls his arm out his grip.

"Don't worry. I'm not planning on hurting her," Ben assures him before walking off. Once everyone else arrives they start with the practise. After they finish, Lizzie heads out with Phoebe.

"I'm starving. Do you want to get something to eat?" Lizzie asks Phoebe.

"I would but I need to find a job," Phoebe says.

"Why?" Lizzie asks.

"Nathan won't pay me anymore until I pay him back for everything else," Phoebe explains.

"Don't worry. I'll pay," Lizzie responds. Jake, Ben, Nathan, Mia, Sam and Evie come out.

"Hey guys, were getting something to eat, do you want to come?" Lizzie asks.

"Sure," Jake says.

"Where's Taylor?" Lizzie asks.

"At the joint, we'll meet him there," Jake replies. They all head off. They arrive at the joint; Taylor goes over to them.

"Hey guys," he says.

"Not working today?" Evie asks.

"No, it's my day off. Let us grab a table," Taylor responds. They all go and sit down. Nathan squeezes himself between Lizzie and Ben, Phoebe smiles to herself.

"What happened to Mia?" She asks Nathan.

"She had plans with Mandy," Nathan responds. Taylor sits on the other side of Lizzie; she smiles at him.

"Hey, so I have some questions about being werewolf," Taylor announces.

"What sort of questions?" Nathan and Jake both ask.

"I read the book Lizzie gave me but there's still somethings it didn't explain. It mentions that we have special abilities, what are they?" Taylor asks.

"We can heal quicker, so don't worry about getting injured," Jake tells him.

"Yes, and we have super hearing. We can hear things from a distance," Nathan says.

"How do you do it?" Taylor asks.

"Close your eyes, pick a certain noise or voice and try to focus on it," Nathan explains. Taylor closes his eyes, after a few minutes he opens his eyes and pulls a disgusted face.

"Disgusting, my dad is making out with someone in the office," Taylor tells them wincing. Everyone laughs.

"Don't worry, you also get super strength, a deadly bite, super speed, night vision," Lizzie informs him.

"What are the negatives?" He asks.

"Turning every full moon," Jake responds.

"And silver, wolfsbane and angel blades weaken you," Lizzie says.

"It doesn't sound so bad," Taylor speaks.

"For now," Nathan tells him. A waiter comes over and takes their orders. Jake leans towards Phoebe.

"Does your brother like Lizzie?" He whispers. Phoebe looks at him.

"I don't think so, why?" She whispers back.

"He's had his arm resting behind her this whole time and he brought her that necklace," Jake says with a hushed voice. Phoebe looks at him surprised and then across the table at Nathan and Lizzie who are laughing together. Lizzie, Sam and Ben arrive back at the house. They walk through the front door and see a random man standing there with five others. Hunter, Alex and Vikki are all tied up. The man looks at them.

"Elizabeth, isn't it? I'm Tyron, I've heard so much about you." he says.

Chapter 10
You Give Werewolves a Bad Name

Everyone stands there looking at each other.

"I'll admit I'm impressed," he says picking up the silver knife.

"Not many people would have dared to take me on," he tells her.

"Yeah well, I'm not most people," Lizzie responds.

"Oh, I know," he replies. He looks at Hunter.

"She is pretty, I'll give you that," he says to his son.

"Let them go," Lizzie declares. He turns his attention to her.

"That's not going to happen. You see I was meant to arrive in town next week, but I decided to come early. Now imagine the shock when I find out that not only is my son living with vampires, but he is also plotting against me with them. Hearing something like that really makes you question your choices as a parent. So here I am, putting an end to this ridiculous fantasy you guys have," Tyron explains. He pulls out a gun and shoots Sam who falls to the floor in pain. Lizzie goes to head over to him, but Ben grabs her and shakes his head. She stops.

"Smart choice," Tyron tells her.

"What was that?" Lizzie asks.

"Vervain," Tyron answers. He shoots it at Ben, but Lizzie catches the bullet.

"Impressive," he says, she stares him down.

"Come now, you didn't think this was my plan did you. No, I know about the other alphas in town Rafael and what is his name? Ah, Michael. Of course. Imagine how poor Taylor must be feeling, not only has he just found out that he is a werewolf and is adjusting to it but he's also going to be thrown into being alpha of a whole pack. It's his dad's fault really, he shouldn't fall for every pretty woman he sees," Tyron announces. Lizzie looks at Ben.

"Go, I'll be fine," she tells him, before Tyron can do anything Ben has already disappeared.

"Let's hope he's not too late," Tyron says. Lizzie looks at Alex he keeps struggling against the ropes.

"Stop bothering, you know there laced with vervain." Tyron reminds him. He pulls out the silver knife and throws it in the fire and then looks at Lizzie.

"I'm not heartless you know, I'm just willing to do what's necessary to make the world safe again," Tyron explains.

"I don't care. Really, I don't. I have met my fair share of people who have wanted to make the world a better place. It's the same story, something happened to them or someone betrayed them, so they go down this vengeful path, quite frankly it's boring. But you know what else they all had in common? In the end they were the only person who inflicted the most danger and pain."

"You can't win by taking out all the supernatural's, there will always be innocent casualties along the way. Okay you're not special somebody has already beat you at this game, you're going to lose," Lizzie tells him. Tyron studies her for a minute.

"My god, you are relentless. You're standing there and you're not frightened of me, you're a warrior and you know if you weren't a vampire, we could have been allies, good ones too. It's a shame I'm going to have to kill you," Tyron tells her. Lizzie looks at him.

"You should have done your research, I'm not just an ordinary vampire. I'm a witch too," Lizzie informs him. She looks at Vikki and then raises her hand two of the men go through the window. Vikki gets out her seat and takes out the other three. Tyron holds his hands up.

"Impressive," he says. Vikki steps towards him, teeth baring. He looks at her.

"Stand down, I'm not going to kill you. Not yet. I'm feeling generous, I hear there's a party next Friday. Let's say we save this until after then," he declares and walks past Lizzie; he goes to the front door.

"I look forward to seeing you again, Elizabeth," he says before leaving. Vikki rushes over to Alex and Hunter to untie them. Lizzie goes over to Sam who is now sitting against the wall clutching his stomach.

"Get it out, I can't heal while it's in there," he tells her.

"This is going to hurt," Lizzie informs him. She uses her magic to get the bullet out, Sam screams. Alex goes over to them and helps Sam up.

"Are you okay?" He asks Sam.

"I am now," Sam tells him. Lizzie goes over to Hunter who looks mortified.

"I'm sorry," he tells her.

"It's not your fault," Lizzie assures him. The front door opens, Ben rushes in with Taylor and his dad. Michael has blood rushing from his side.

"Lizzie, help him. He's dying," Taylor announces, they lie him on the sofa. Michael clutches his side.

"Taylor, listen to me," he tries saying. Taylor takes his hand.

"What's wrong?" Taylor asks.

"I know. I've known this whole time, you never told me because you thought I'd be ashamed, but I knew. I want you to know…that I could never be ashamed of you…but instead, I'm proud," Michael tells him trying to catch his breath. Everyone looks at Lizzie who has just froze.

"Lizzie!" Taylor says looking at her with tears in his eyes. Hunter notices.

"Behind the house there are some red flowers, go and get them," Hunter says. Alex, Sam and Ben just look at him.

"Now!" Hunter demands. Sam and Ben rush outside. Hunter goes over to Taylor with a cloth, he hands it to him.

"Put pressure on the wound," he tells him. Taylor does. Hunter walks over to Lizzie; he grabs her arms.

"Lizzie!" He says. Lizzie doesn't notice, she's just staring. Hunter looks at Alex just as Ben and Sam return with the flowers. Hunter hands Vikki a bowl, he puts the flowers in it.

"Mash it together, and fast," he orders. Vikki does, she hands the bowl back to him a few minutes later. Hunter does a quick a spell and then hands it to Michael.

"Drink it, you will feel better," he says. Michael drinks it and within minutes his wound has healed, and he sits up.

"Thank you," he says to Hunter. He looks across the room at Lizzie and notices her skin developing burns.

"Is she okay?" He asks everyone. They all look over.

"Oh, my God," Alex says, he rushes towards her, but Hunter holds his hand up.

"Don't," he tells him. Alex looks at him. "It's poison," Hunter responds.

"What do you mean poison?" Sam asks. Hunter looks at Lizzie and then at the fireplace.

"He knew. My dad. He knew she was a witch, and he knew she'd use her magic, he was counting on it," Hunter informs them.

"What? How could you possibly know that?" Ben asks.

"The knife we made; it was designed to kill an alpha, but a witch had to use it. Lizzie used her blood to make it, they were connected, so when he chucked it in the fire the spell took a toll. The silver weakens a wolf but when made by a witch's blood, it can be used as a poison to stop them. All she had to do was a spell to activate it," Hunter explains.

"Is that why she's frozen?" Taylor asks.

"He's weakened her," Hunter answers. Alex rolls his eyes and touches Lizzie.

"NO!" Hunter yells. Lizzie lets out a scream, a powerful surge vibrates around the room. All the vampires cover their ears. Michael gets up.

"Make it stop!" Sam yells over the scream.

"I don't know how," Hunter tells him. Michael snaps Lizzies neck and catches her in his arms. Everyone gets up and looks at him.

"What? She's a vampire, she'll be fine," He tells them putting her on the sofa.

"What does it mean? Is she in danger?" Alex asks.

"I don't know," Hunter answers.

"Is she going to be, okay?" Sam asks.

"I don't know," Hunter replies.

"Do you know anything?" Ben asks.

"I know that you're all going to die if my father gets his own way," Hunter responds before walking out the room. Taylor and Michael leave.

"I'm going to bed. See you up there," Vikki says to Alex before going upstairs.

"Someone should stay with her," Alex declares to the boys.

"I'll do it," Ben replies.

"Are you sure?" Sam questions.

"Yeah, you need to rest since you got shot, and your girlfriend is waiting for you upstairs," Ben tells them.

"He makes a very good point. Goodnight," Sam says before leaving.

"If anything happens or she wakes…" Alex starts.

"I'll come and get you," Ben finishes for him. Alex looks at him before leaving. Once everyone has left, Ben grabs a blanket and puts it over Lizzie, he kisses her on the forehead and then goes and sits on the sofa opposite. A few hours later Lizzie wakes, she sees Ben sleeping. She looks over at the clock, it reads three. Lizzie gets up and walks towards the front door, she looks back at Ben before leaving.

An hour later Hunter wakes Ben up.

"What?" Ben asks.

"Lizzie's gone, weren't you supposed to be watching her?" Hunter asks. Ben jumps up.

"We need to find her," Hunter tells him. Alex and Sam come downstairs.

"Oh look, sleeping beauty's awake," Alex says.

"Where do we start?" Ben asks.

"The woods," Sam answers.

"Have you seen how big the woods are? There's only four of us," Ben declares.

"Make that eight," Elliot says walking through the doors with his brothers. Ben sighs.

"Great, you may as well just sniff her out?" Ben says sarcastically.

"We wouldn't have to if you didn't neglect your duties," Nathan points out. They stare each other down.

"Alright, enough already! The important thing right now is my sister, so put your childish arguments to the side for one night," Alex tells them before heading outside. Everyone follows.

"We'll go in twos. Me and Sam. Rafael and Elliot. Ben and Erik. Nathan and Hunter. Any questions?" Alex asks. They all shake their heads.

"Good," Alex speaks before heading one way. Everyone heads off. Nathan and Hunter are walking through the woods.

"Why doesn't Ben like you?" Hunter questions.

"I honestly couldn't tell you, but I bet it has something to do with Lizzie. Same as you," Nathan responds.

"What do you mean?" Hunter asks.

"Ben strikes me as the jealous type. Lizzie and I are close, and I don't think he likes that very much. He doesn't like you because you care for Lizzie, even if you won't admit it," Nathan explains. Hunter grabs Nathans arm.

"Do you hear that?" He asks him. Nathan stops and looks at him, he shakes his head. Hunter puts a finger to his mouth. Nathan listens carefully. He can hear the wind.

"What is it?" He asks Hunter.

"It's Lizzie," Hunter replies. He runs in a direction, Nathan follows. After a short while, they stop.

"Well, where is she?" Nathan asks. Hunter looks at him panting.

"I don't know," he responds. Nathan takes a deep breath; his eyes turn blue and he faces Hunter. He takes a step towards him before stopping.

"Lizzie!" he shouts, his eyes go back to normal. He walks past Hunter. Lying on the floor is an unconscious Lizzie, Nathan bends down next to her.

"She's been bit," Hunter tells him looking at her leg, Nathan looks.

"No," he says. He bites his wrist and gives the blood to Lizzie.

"Come on Lizzie, wake up," He pleads holding her in his arms. Hunter bends down on the other side of her.

"Please, you can't leave me here with all these idiots," Nathan says. Lizzie gasps and jolts up. Nathan sighs in relief hugging her.

"You are okay love, I got you," he tells her. They sit there for a minute, Lizzie collapse back in his arms. He picks her up.

"Let's get you home," Nathan speaks walking off. Hunter follows.

Back at the house, everyone else gathers on the lawn.

"We couldn't find her," Erik says.

"Us either," Rafael responds. Alex sighs.

"She has to be somewhere; a person doesn't just disappear," he says with a raised voice. He starts getting agitated.

"Alex," Sam says, he grabs his arm and points towards the trees where Nathan emerges with her. Alex sighs in relief.

"It's okay, she's okay," Nathan informs them.

"Get her inside," Alex demands. Nathan heads up the stairs with her.

"Where was she?" Alex asks Hunter.

"Lying in the woods, for dead. Somebody bit her," Hunter informs them before going inside. Everyone looks at Rafael.

"Don't look at me," he tells them, he walks off. Alex goes inside and heads upstairs. He stops at Lizzies door and peaks through. Nathan is putting her in bed.

"I won't let anyone hurt you again. This I promise you, love; I would kill anybody that ever thought of brining you pain," Nathan says quietly while tucking her in. Alex smiles to himself.

"I can hear you breathing you know," Nathan informs him turning around. Alex comes into the room.

"I was just coming to check on her," he tells him.

"She should be out for the rest of the night," Nathan responds.

"Okay, I guess I'll leave you to it. She's in good hands," Alex replies before leaving. Nathan turns back to look at Lizzie one last time before leaving.

Chapter 11
The Dream

Lizzie wakes up the next morning and goes downstairs. Sam, Alex, Vikki, Hunter and Ben are in the living room.

"Good morning," Vikki says.

"Morning, I had such a weird dream last night. I was in the woods and Nathan and Hunter were there," Lizzie tells them. They all look at her.

"It wasn't a dream, was it?" She asks. They shake their heads.

"No, Lizzie do you remember anything?" Alex asks.

"No. I don't even know how I got there, or back here actually," Lizzie answers.

"Nathan brought you back. He even tucked you in," Hunter informs her.

"Really?" Lizzie asks.

"Oh yeah, the only thing he missed was the bedtime story," Hunter replies grinning.

At the Rodriguez, Nathan enters the study room.

"We heard you found Lizzie last night, how is she?" Phoebe asks.

"Perfectly fine now," Nathan assures them.

"Do you know what she was doing in the woods?" Heather asks.

"No, but we know she wasn't alone. Whoever was with her, bit her and nearly killed her," Nathan answers.

"Have you asked her who?" Erik questions.

"What is this, an interrogation? No, I haven't spoken to her yet. She has work later. If you guys are so worried about her, why don't you just ask her yourself?" Nathan queries before storming out.

"What is his problem?" Phoebe asks.

"Who knows," Erik responds.

"I think it has something to do with Lizzie," Heather replies.

"What do you mean?" Elliot asks.

"You guys are seriously telling me you've never noticed before?" Heather asks.

"Noticed what?" Erik questions.

"Nathan has some pretty strong feelings for her," Heather says.

"Oh, for God's sake. Not another one," Rafael moans getting up and leaving.

Lizzie is lying across the sofa; Ben is sitting next to her. Her head is on a pillow on his lap. Alex, Vikki and Sam are sitting on the other sofa. Hunter is on the stairs.

"I want to know something," Vikki says. Lizzie turns her head to look at her.

"What's that?" She asks her.

"What was your relationship like with Nathan when you lived with them. He's the only one we don't actually know about," Vikki responds. Lizzie thinks for a minute.

"We were close. He taught me how to hunt bunnies. I cried over it," Lizzie replies.

"I want to hear this story," Sam says sitting back. Lizzie smiles.

"There's not much to tell," Lizzie responds.

Flashback to 1875

Nathan and Lizzie are by a lake, Nathan is holding a dead bunny.

"See, it's that easy. Now you try," he says to her while wiping the blood from his face. Lizzie looks at him then disappears into the distance. She arrives back a few minutes later holding a dead bunny, blood around her mouth. She walks past Nathan and hands him the bunny. He starts grinning as she sits down on the nearby bench.

"That wasn't hard, was it?" Nathan asks, he turns around as Lizzie starts crying. She's got her back to him; he drops the bunny.

"Come now love, it's just a bunny. I'm sure it didn't feel any pain," Nathan tells her.

"It's not just the bunny, it's everything. I am a monster. I left my family at a time we should have stuck together. I can't find them; I tried looking before I met you guys. They could probably be dead right now and I was selfish enough to run away, I bet they hate me," Lizzie cries. Nathan looks out over the lake before walking towards her.

"That's not true. Nobody could hate you; you are amazing. You are the most caring and considerate person I've ever met, and I've been around a long time. Anybody who hates you is an idiot; they don't see how perfect you are. We all make mistakes Elizabeth; we must learn to forgive ourselves before asking for others forgiveness. I promise you that as long as you have me around, you'll be safe. I'd never let any harm come to you," Nathan assures her, he wipes her tears.

"You really mean that?" She asks.

"More than you could possibly know," Nathan responds. Lizzie looks out across the water and notices the sun setting.

"The suns setting," she tells him. He looks over.

"So, it is," He responds. He stands up and holds his hand out.

"We should go, my brother will start to get worried," Nathan informs her. She takes his hand and gets up. They leave.

Back to present day.

"He has always been protective. It's one of the things that draws girls to him," Lizzie says.

"Have you ever been drawn to him?" Hunter asks.

"Nope. He's got a thing for blondes, which is why he's going to the ball on Friday with Mia," Lizzie answers. She sits up. "I have to get going. Can't be late. I'll see you all later," she declares before leaving.

Lizzie arrives at work.

"Morning, glad to see you looking better," Taylor tells her.

"Sorry about yesterday. I know you needed my help," Lizzie responds.

"Don't worry about it. You weren't yourself," Taylor says. Lizzie goes over to him behind the bar.

"Did it make you feel better about yourself?" She asks. Taylor looks at her confused. She notices.

"That your dad knew you were gay. You never told anyone because you didn't want it getting back to him in fear of his reaction, but he told last night that he was proud of you anyway," Lizzie explains.

"How, how did you know?" Taylor stammers.

"It was obvious. You have great fashion sense and you are great with advice. Plus, I've seen you checking guys out," Lizzie informs him.

"Oh, well I am glad that he loves me regardless but if I'm honest I was more worried about someone else finding out," Taylor says.

"You mean Jake. You're scared that if he knows, he'll figure out that you have feelings for him," Lizzie responds.

"How could you possibly know all of that?" Taylor asks mortified. Lizzie laughs.

"I read your mind," Lizzie says.

"You can do that?" Taylor questions.

"No, I'm just good at picking things up. It's a witch thing," Lizzie answers.

"What's a witch thing?" Erik asks going over.

"Good morning, Erik, it's good to see you too," Lizzie says. Erik looks at her.

"I know it is," he responds. Lizzie just ignores him. Taylor laughs.

"We were just talking about boys," Taylor tells him.

"Boys in general or a certain boy named Jake?" Erik asks. They both look at him.

"What?" Taylor queries.

"Relax, your secret is safe with me," he assures him. Taylor looks at Lizzie for help.

"Don't look at me, he's always been weird," Lizzie says before walking out to wait a table. Taylor looks at Erik.

"Were you worried about her?" He asks him.

"Yes, Lizzie has always been a dear friend of mine. Her safety worries me sometimes," Erik answers.

"Well, don't worry. She's perfectly fine and safe," Taylor assures him before leaving too. Erik looks at Lizzie who is talking to some customers.

At the Rodriguez, Heather and Elliot are in the study room together.

"What's wrong?" Heather asks him. Elliot looks at her.

"I'm just thinking," he answers.

"About?" Heather asks.

"Last night. Nathan found Lizzie in the woods bitten. It wasn't a full moon which means it had to of been somebody who was half werewolf. That could be anyone in this family or Hunter. I know it wasn't Hunter, he might not show it, but he cares for her. Erik and Phoebe adore her, they wouldn't hurt her. She saved our child's life; we have no reason to hurt her and if what you say about Nathan is true, then it wasn't him," Elliot explains.

"That leaves Rafael," Heather says.

"Which just seems too obvious. Plus, he looked us in the eye last night and said he didn't do it. I don't believe he'd lie to us, again," Elliot tells her.

"So, what do you think happened?" Heather asks.

"I don't know, but we need to find out," Elliot responds.

At the joint, Lizzie heads into the storage room, she looks at the shelves of wine and sighs. She holds her hand out and murmurs something, nothing happens.

"What's wrong?" Nathan asks appearing at the door. She jumps startled then looks at him.

"Nothing, why do you think somethings wrong?" She questions. He steps into the room and closes the door.

"You can't fool me love. I know when somethings wrong," Nathan responds. She looks at him.

"It's my magic. It's not working properly, and I don't know why," Lizzie tells him. Nathan goes over to a rack and pulls a wine bottle of, he places it on the table in front of her and then goes and stands behind her.

"Just concentrate, bring the bottle to you. Take a deep breath," Nathan says. Lizzie takes a breath and looks at the bottle. She holds her hand out, the bottle shakes and then breaks bursting everywhere. Lizzie looks defeated, Nathan notices. He goes and stands in front of her taking her hands.

"Lizzie, look at me. It's fine. Everybody has off days, we all know that you can do magic. Don't worry about it. Your magic isn't what makes you and you don't need it to prove anything. I know how strong you are without it. We can figure this out, it's not a problem," Nathan assures her. She looks at him.

"But who am I without my magic?" She questions.

"The same person you've always been, Elizabeth Jones," Nathan assures her. Just then the door opens, and Taylor walks in.

"Sorry to interrupt, but we have customers," he reminds her.

"Yeah, I'm coming," she says heading off with him. That night Lizzie is tossing and turning, she's dreaming about the school. It's dark and there are three cars crashed together. The people from them are screaming as they get attacked. Lizzie shoots up panting. It's morning outside, Lizzie gets up and goes downstairs. Sam is waiting for her.

"Hey, were meeting Evie along the way," he tells her.

"That's cool," Lizzie says. They open the door, Phoebe and Erik are there.

"We thought we'd walk with you," Erik speaks grinning. Sam and Lizzie look at each other before leaving. On their way, they pick up Evie and Taylor appears.

"I'm telling you, it felt so real," Lizzie declares as they head towards the gates. Sam and Evie are walking behind the other four. They turn the corner to the gates.

"Maybe because it was," Erik announces. They look at the parking lot, it has three cars crashed together and blood everywhere. The police are taking pictures, Lizzie freezes.

"Did I do this?" She asks with a shaky breath.

"No, I'm sure you didn't," Phoebe responds.

"Did you guys hear. They found the bodies five people were killed," Brooke says going over to Evie. Lizzie steps back, Erik and Taylor grab her. Phoebe looks at Sam.

"Get her out of here," she demands. Sam pulls Lizzie's arm.

"Lizzie, come on. Let's go home," he says pulling her away.

Back at the Jones, Alex is having a meeting with Vikki, Ben, Hunter, Rafael, Elliot, Heather and Nathan.

"We need to do something," Alex tells them.

"Like what? He destroyed our weapon and everything we need to make it again," Hunter reminds him.

"We have to think of something," Alex responds.

"I have an idea," Rafael announces.

"You do?" Elliot asks.

"Yes, we could just leave town," Rafael says.

"That is not an option. Some of us actually like it here," Nathan tells him.

"Suit yourself then," Rafael replies.

"Moving on, what if…" Alex starts. The front door opens, Sam walks through with Lizzie.

"Why aren't you in school?" Vikki asks.

"There was an attack," Sam answers.

"We saw it on the news, they haven't shut the school," Alex responds. Sam looks at Lizzie.

"Lizzie had a dream, about the attack. When she woke up this morning, it was real," Sam informs them. They all look at Lizzie.

"I did that, I killed all those innocent people. Why would I do that?" Lizzie asks looking completely distraught. She doesn't look at anyone.

"Lizzie, we don't know that. It could have just been a coincidence. You were here last night," Ben tells her.

"No, no. It's happening. I knew it would," she says.

"What's she going on about?" Heather asks confused. Alex and Sam shrug and Nathan sighs.

"Ever since that night in the woods, Lizzie has been feeling different," Nathan says.

"Stop, you promised," Lizzie declares. Nathan looks away from her and gets up.

"Her powers have stopped working, she's not the same. Her vampire side is taking over and because she hasn't fed in years, it's going to be bad," Nathan tells them. Lizzie looks at him, feeling betrayed.

"How could you?" She asks. Nathan looks at her.

"I'm sorry love, they needed to know," he answers.

"That wasn't your decision to make," Lizzie replies. Just then the front door swings open, Tyron walks in.

"Hello again," he says. Lizzie takes a step away from him.

"Elizabeth, you look, sad. Is everything okay? Oh wait, don't tell me, your powers aren't working," Tyron says grinning. Lizzie glares at him.

"What do you want?" Alex asks.

"I just thought I'd drop by. Say hello. Check in on my favourite vampire. It is a vampire now, isn't it?" He questions Lizzie.

"You are enjoying this, aren't you?" Hunter asks.

"Oh yes, I never thought I could have so much fun messing up someone's life," Tyron answers.

"Why? What are you getting out of this?" Rafael asks.

"Not me, Elizabeth. I'm just showing you what you truly are deep down. You may be a witch, but you were a vampire first, and a vampire's instinct always wins. You're a predator of the night, a monster," Tyron announces. He puts his hand in his pocket and pulls out a bottle.

"Do you know what this is?" He asks her. She shakes her head.

"It's a lobelia flower. It took me a while, but I found some. The only thing that can weaken a witch," He informs her, Lizzie starts to feel lightheaded. She grabs the wall.

"It's starting to hit you isn't it. I won't lie, it was hard to get it in your system. That bite the other night did it though, it even removed your memory, so you wouldn't remember who did it," he says, he looks over at her and then at the rest of the group.

"Did you know too much could actually kill a witch. Now I wasn't there when she was bit, but I'm getting the feeling that she has way too much in her system to keep her alive. Afterall, she doesn't look too good," Tyron informs them. They all look at Lizzie, who's having a hard time standing.

Nathan runs over to her as she falls to the floor. Everyone gathers round.

"Lizzie, stay with us," Nathan says as Tyron disappears.

"Nathan," Lizzie whispers before her eyes close.

"We have to get it out her system," Hunter announces.

"How?" Alex asks.

"Take her to her room. It's not going to be pretty," Hunter says. Nathan picks her up and heads up the stairs.

"Why's he going after Lizzie?" Heather asks.

"Because she's the strongest. He knows he would have lost if she went against him, so he took her out," Hunter explains before heading upstairs too.

Upstairs, Nathan has put Lizzie on the bed, Hunter enters the room followed by the boys. He looks at everyone.

"I need two buckets, rope and a knife," he tells them.

"What's the knife for?" Ben asks.

"To cut her open. The only way to save her, is to drain her. Lobelia is different from everything else. It's going to sting and she's going to scream. Which is why we will tie her down with rope," Hunter explains. Sam and Ben leave the room.

"I will warn you; she's going to be going through an extreme amount of pain in a minute. If you don't think you can watch it, I suggest you leave," he informs them.

"I'm going nowhere," Alex responds.

"Okay fine. I'll do the cutting. Alex, you and Sam can hold her down. Elliot and Rafael, you're in charge of the buckets," Hunter instructs.

"What about me and Nathan?" Ben asks coming into the room.

"I'm kicking you both out," Hunter replies.

"Why?" Ben questions.

"One, because you like her. And two, I don't like you," Hunter says to Ben.

"I'm not leaving her," Nathan warns him.

"Nathan, she'll be fine. I'm here, as are her brothers. She's in good hands," Elliot tells him. Nathan looks at Hunter before walking out. Ben follows.

They head into the living room where Heather and Vikki are. Phoebe and Erik come through the door.

"Why aren't you in school?" Nathan asks them.

"Everyone was told to leave early because of the investigation," Erik answers.

"Where's Lizzie?" Phoebe questions. As soon as she asks that the lights start flickering and they can hear faint screaming. They look at everyone.

"It's a long story," Vikki tells them.

After a while, Hunter, Elliot, Rafael and Sam all come down.

"Will she be okay now?" Vikki asks.

"Yeah, she's just resting. Alex is with her," Hunter answers. Nathan gets up and goes upstairs. Alex is sitting on the bed next to Lizzie, he looks at Nathan as he walks in.

"Can I ask you something?" He asks.

"Sure," Nathan replies.

"You have some strong feelings for my sister, why haven't you ever told her?" Alex questions. Nathan looks at her.

"Because she's in love with somebody else," he tells him.

"How do you know it's love with Ben. Afterall it was your name she called out before she passed out," Alex reminds him. Nathan looks at him before leaving.

Chapter 12
Fight with the Hunters

Two days later, Lizzie slowly starts to wake she looks around and sees Heather sitting next to her dabbing a wet towel on her head.

"Heather," she says sitting up.

"Careful, you had a fever. We didn't think you were going to make it," Heather tells her.

"Where is everyone?" Lizzie asks.

"They're gone. You've been out two days. Tyron found out you were still alive. The boys have gone to fight him in the woods," Heather explains. Lizzie looks out the window, it's dark.

"We have to go help them," Lizzie says.

"We can't, they told us to stay here," Heather responds. Lizzie looks at her.

"I don't care, they aren't coming back alive. It was the whole point. They're being betrayed by one of their own. Heather, we have to save them," Lizzie informs them. Just then there's a crash downstairs. Heather and Lizzie look at each other.

"Phoebe and Vikki are down there," Heather tells her. They leave the room. They run downstairs, the big guy from the joint is there with three others. Phoebe is being help by her throat against the wall by him. The other three have Vikki.

"I won't ask again, where's the witch?" The bigger one says to Phoebe.

"Right here," Lizzie declares. He turns around dropping Phoebe.

"Collum frangeretur," Lizzie says waving her fist. All of the guy's necks break, and they fall to the floor. Lizzie and Heather go over to the girls.

"Are you okay?" Lizzie asks helping Vikki up.

"Yeah," Vikki replies. Lizzie looks at Phoebe who nods.

"Good because we have to go," Lizzie responds, they all leave the house.

Deep in the woods, Elliot gets thrown against the tree.

"I can do this all night," Tyron shouts. Alex gets up off the floor.

"Someone's up for round two," Tyron tells his men who chuckle.

"Dad," A voice says. Elliot looks up and sees his son there.

"Henry, what are you doing? Get out of here!" Elliot demands.

"He can't," Rafael says getting up, everyone looks at him.

"Oh, come on now. You didn't actually think I was on your side, did you?" Rafael asks.

"What? Why?" Elliot asks.

"Tyron offered me a way to kill Lizzie, I took it. I just had to make a sacrifice first," Rafael answers looking at Henry.

"No, not my son," Elliot yells running at him. They fight, Rafael throws Elliot back.

"Give it up Elliot, you can't beat me. I'm an alpha and I am victorious!" Rafael shouts raising his arms and looking up. All of a suddenly he goes flying. Lizzie lands on her knees, hand on the floor. She looks up; her eyes are green, and her fangs are showing. She stands, the girls appear behind her. Rafael gets up of the ground. Tyron looks at her.

"Elizabeth Jones, welcome to the battle," he says chuckling. He looks at his men and signals for them to attack. Lizzie looks at the girls.

"Go, we got this," Vikki tells her. Lizzie disappears and the girls start fighting. Rafael turns to look at his brothers.

"It was you. You were the one who bit Lizzie in the woods," Nathan declares.

"Yes, and if you had only found her a few minutes later, she would have been dead," Rafael replies.

"Why? What do you need my son for? He's innocent," Elliot responds.

"For now, I will help him tap into his werewolf side. You see, everyone has a weakness. Lizzie would never hurt a kid, especially not Elliot's. Once I realised that, it became clear, Henry can kill her, she won't fight him," Rafael informs them.

"He won't do it. He's a good kid," Elliot says. Rafael smiles and bends down over Elliot.

"If he doesn't do it, I'll kill him," Rafael informs him. He snaps Elliot's neck and gets up and snaps his brothers. He walks towards Henry who takes a step back.

"You don't need to be scared of me Henry, I'm here to help," Rafael says.

"I don't trust you and I won't help you," Henry declares.

"Fine, suit yourself," Rafael responds, he bares his teeth at Henry.

"No!" Lizzie yells, she pushes Henry out the way and runs at Rafael. He sends her flying. Lizzie sits up, her arm has been bit. Rafael proceeds towards Henry.

"Clypeus," Lizzie says, she spreads her hand out over to Henry, a shield appears around him. Rafael grins and then walks towards Lizzie.

"I am getting so sick and tired of you and your tricks," He announces kicking her away, she spits out blood.

"Now, I am going to have to kill you and no one can stop me," he informs her. Lizzie looks across the woods. Elliot, Nathan, Erik and Sam unconscious. Ben, Alex, Vikki and Phoebe are fighting. She sees Heather go to her child.

"Come on baby, we need to go. It's not safe," she tells him.

"No, Mum you can't. He'll kill her. You have to help. She saved my life, twice," Henry responds. Heather looks over where Lizzie is, she's struggling on the floor against Rafael.

"Go, wake your dad," Heather says to Henry. He goes over to Elliot. Rafael punches Lizzie. She tries to fight back.

"There's no point. Your too weak. I'll admit, it was brave to come out here when you weren't fully recovered. Brave but foolish," he tells her.

"You're the foolish one," Lizzie responds trying to catch her breath. Rafael chuckles.

"That bite looks nasty," he says. Lizzie looks at her arm and then back at him. She raises her other arm, he grabs it.

"I don't think so," he declares. Suddenly his face winces, blood spills out his mouth. He drops Lizzie's arm and turns round. There's a branch sticking out his back. Heather is standing there. He falls to his knees. Elliot wakes along with his brothers and Sam. Everyone else rushes over to them.

"Why?" Rafael asks her.

"You put my sons' life in danger one too many times and I can't let you do it again," she answers before shoving her hand in his chest, she rips his heart out. He crashes on the floor.

"NOO!" Phoebe screams. Hunter and Vikki grab her as she tumbles to the ground sobbing. Lizzie gets up off the floor and goes and stands next to Heather, they look at each other.

Chapter 13
The Ball

"What have you done?" Tyron asks angrily. Heather and Lizzie turn to look at everyone else. Phoebe's still on the floor crying. Elliot is with Henry and his brothers.

"What needed to be done," Heather responds.

"You killed him," Erik says.

"He was going to kill Lizzie and my son. I made a choice, and I won't apologise for it," Heather tells him. Erik walks over to Phoebe.

"Phoebe come on. Get up," he says dragging her up and hugging her. Tyron looks at Lizzie walking to the middle of everyone.

"You! This is all your fault. People will continue to die because of you, you don't see it now, but you will. Everyone you love will slowly die over time and it will all be down to you. Loving you is a curse within itself," he tells her. Heather grabs Lizzie's arm and pulls her away.

On Friday afternoon, the door knocks, Sam gets it and Nathan walks in eating chips.

"I was hungry," Nathan says sitting on the sofa. Sam joins them.

"Where's the girls?" Nathan asks.

"Vikki's already left and Lizzie's upstairs," Sam answers. Lizzie comes running downstairs.

"I'm starving," she announces going over and standing behind Nathan, who's sitting on the sofa. She leans over and takes some of his chips. He looks up at her and she smiles at him.

"Ahem," Alex speaks. They both look at him.

"Don't you have somewhere to be?" He asks Lizzie.

"Oh yeah, the Christmas ball," Lizzie responds running out the house. The boys smile as she goes. Ben goes to head out too.

"Woah, where are you going?" Sam asks.

"To get something, don't worry. I'll be back in time for the ball," Ben tells them before walking out.

Lizzie arrives at the hall and heads upstairs where all the other girls are.

"Lizzie, finally. Where have you been?" The mayor asks.

"I'm sorry. I lost track of time," Lizzie answers. She heads over to Phoebe, Heather and Vikki.

"Hey, how are you?" She asks Phoebe.

"I'm okay. I wasn't at first, but I understand why Rafael had to die, he was dangerous, and he was hurting people. Someone had to do something about it," Phoebe replies. Lizzie hugs her.

"Let's see your dress. Phoebe says it is jaw dropping," Heather tells her. Lizzie smiles.

"It's not that great," she responds.

"Oh, please. Nathan was speechless and he's never speechless," Phoebe says.

"Well, that's not true. Mia made him pretty speechless last night," Mandy speaks going over.

"I almost forgot you were here," Phoebe replies. Mandy smiles and then looks at Lizzie.

"Come on then, let's see this dress that is so amazing," She announces.

"Do you seriously have nothing better to do then stand here being annoying?" Vikki asks.

"I can think of a few things. Speaking of who is everyone being escorted by? My boyfriend is drop dead gorgeous," Many declares.

"You have a boyfriend?" Phoebe asks repulsed. Mandy looks at her.

"Yes, try not to steal this one," she responds before walking off, pushing past Evie and Brooke.

"She is a piece of work," Heather announces.

"Tell us about it," Evie says going over.

"Who are you going with?" Lizzie asks Brooke.

"Taylor, we both needed someone," Brooke answers.

"Isn't he a chosen representer to?" Heather asks.

"Yes, you can go with someone who is representing their household too," Brooke tells them.

"Speaking off, who's taking over Rafael place?" Evie questions.

"Elliot, it went down to the next oldest," Phoebe replies.

"So, you and Jake. How did that happen?" Brooke asks her to try to change subject.

"It was at his party. We just spent a lot of time together," Phoebe responds.

"Mia will probably hate you now," Brooke informs her.

"Don't worry, I can handle myself," Phoebe assures her. Sometime later, everyone is getting ready as the boys arrive.

The girls all head to the top of the balcony where the boys await.

"Where's Ben?" Vikki asks Lizzie. She looks at her.

"I don't know," she answers. Alex goes over with Elliot and Jake.

"Ladies, you all look gorgeous," Elliot tells them.

"We know," Phoebe responds. The girls chuckle.

"Is Ben not with you?" Lizzie asks Alex.

"No, he left a few hours ago. He said he'd be here though," he informs her. Lizzie looks across the banister where Nathan is standing with Mia. The mayor comes up.

"Three minutes until were starting," she warns them and then goes back down. Heather and Elliot walk off to join the group. Lizzie looks towards the door.

"Hey, don't stress. It looks like Mandy's date didn't show either," Phoebe tells her.

"Speak of the devil," Vikki whispers as she heads over to them.

"Who do we have here?" She asks looking at Alex.

"I'm Alex. Lizzie's older brother," Alex responds. She looks him up and down.

"Huh, you must feel left out. Both your brothers are good looking and then there's, you," Mandy says looking at Lizzie.

"I'd be careful if I were you, Mandy. I hear accidents happen a lot on these stairs, you wouldn't want to fall and embarrass yourself in front of the whole town," Lizzie replies.

"Was a threat?" Mandy asks.

"Of course not. It was a warning," Lizzie answers. Mandy storms off. They hear the mayor shout one more minute.

"We should head over to everyone," Jake says to Phoebe. She takes his arm, and they leave. Ben walks through the door and heads up the stairs.

"There you are! Where were you?" Mandy questions going over to him.

"Sorry, I had to make a stop first," Ben informs her.

"Never mind, you're here now. It's about to start," Mandy speaks pulling him over to everyone.

"Is he serious?" Vikki asks.

"I'll kill him," Alex says stepping forward. Lizzie stops him.

"No, leave him. It's fine. Go join everyone," Lizzie tells them. They both look at her.

"Are you sure? What about you?" Alex asks.

"I'll be fine, go on," she answers. They look at her before heading over. Alex looks down the stairs and sees Hunter arriving. The music begins. Everyone lines up at the top of the stairs. Hunter catches Alex gaze. Alex signals his head towards Lizzie who is by herself on the other side. The first couple get announced and Lizzie goes back into the room. She walks over to the window and looks out it, she hears the door open.

"Alex, I said I was fine," she says turning around, she sees Hunter standing there. He extends his arm.

"Shall we?" He asks her. She smiles and takes his arm; they head out just as the announcer says her name. They head down the staircase and into the ballroom to join the other couples. The music starts and everyone begins dancing. Lizzie looks at Hunter.

"I thought you said dances were lame," she says.

"They are, but then I realised that I would never forgive myself if I missed out on the chance to dance with a beautiful woman," Hunter responds. Lizzie laughs, she looks up and sees Ben and Mandy together. Hunter notices.

"I think he's an idiot. You are definitely the best dressed here and he's missing out on the chance to be seen with you," Hunter says.

"I don't think he'll see it like that," Lizzie replies. Hunter spins her out as they switch partners. Nathan appears and takes her hands, they start dancing.

"So, how come you didn't come with Ben?" Nathan asks.

"He's dating Mandy and decided to go with her," Lizzie answers. Nathan nods.

"Was Hunter the only person left?" He asks. Lizzie looks at him.

"No, that's not what it's like. Hunter stepped in when I had no one. He's been a really good friend these past few days, unlike some people," Lizzie responds.

"Are you sure it's just friends?" He queries.

"What is your problem? It's not like we were ever more than friends, not like you and Mia. You and Ben have a lot in common, you both know how to hide a relationship," Lizzie declares before storming out. She heads outside and goes over to the fountain. There's snow falling, she sits down and looks into the water. She hears footsteps approaching and looks up, she sees Nathan walking towards her. Lizzie rolls her eyes and looks back into the water, he goes and sits next to her.

"Lizzie?" He says, she does not acknowledge him. He takes her hand. "Lizzie, please. Tell me what's wrong," He pleads. Lizzie looks at him.

"Are you with Mia?" She asks.

"Yes," Nathan answers.

"How long?" Lizzie questions.

"Two weeks," Nathan replies.

"And did you tell me?" Lizzie queries.

"No," Nathan says ashamed. Lizzie looks away.

"You should go back, your girlfriends probably waiting for you," she tells him.

"I don't get it, why are you so upset about it? You wanted Ben," Nathan reminds her.

"What are you going on about? I thought Ben liked me, he lied. I'm not upset that you're with Mia, you're allowed to have girlfriends. I'm upset that you never told me, and I had to hear it from Mandy, of all people. I thought we could tell each other anything," Lizzie declares. Nathan looks at her.

"You have no idea, do you?" He asks.

"Idea? What do you mean?" Lizzie questions. Nathan scoffs and stands up, Lizzie follows. He looks at her.

"Do you have any idea how hard it's been for me? I've had to keep myself under control whenever you're around. I don't want Mia; I don't even like her," Nathan says with a raised voice.

"Then why are you with her?" Lizzie asks.

"Because I can't have you," Nathan answers. They both go silent and look at each other.

"What did you just say?" Lizzie asks. Nathan sighs.

"I can't have you. Lizzie, I have been in love with you since the first time we met. I can't get you out of my head, I can't stop worrying about you every minute of the day, I just want to be with you. But I can't. I can't because you're in love with someone else and that hurts more than anything has ever hurt before. I had to watch you fall in love with my brother, and now I'm watching you fall in love with somebody who doesn't deserve you," Nathan responds. Lizzie stands there for a minute looking at him.

"You're in love with me?" She asks. Nathan nods.

"Yes, I'm in love with you, I have been for ninety-one years. But you never noticed," Nathan says before turning and walking off.

After hours of dancing and speeches, everyone heads home. Lizzie, Alex, Hunter, Sam and Vikki all arrive home.

"I am tired so I will be going to bed," Vikki announces. She kisses Alex.

"I'll be up in a minute," he tells her as she leaves the room. Sam heads upstairs as Ben walks through the door, they look at him.

"Hey," he says sheepishly.

"Do you want us to stay?" Alex asks her. Lizzie shakes her head.

"No, I'm going to go up to bed anyway," she responds. Alex and Hunter leave the room, Lizzie goes to follow.

"Lizzie, wait. Please," Ben says. Lizzie stops on the stairs and turns around.

"Ben, it's been a long night. Full of surprises. We don't have to do this. You're with Mandy, and your happy. We can leave it at that," Lizzie informs him.

"What about us? Where does that leave us?" Ben asks. Lizzie looks at him.

"We remain friends, like before," Lizzie answers before heading up the stairs. After the new year, Sam and Lizzie are sitting in the living room, Hunter comes down.

"Why not? It will be fun," Sam declares.

"I don't want to," Lizzie responds.

"What's this?" Hunter asks going over and sitting on the other sofa.

"Holiday," Sam answers. He looks at them.

"Alex, Vikki and Sam are going on holiday in the summer," Lizzie explains.

"And you don't want to go?" Hunter asks.

"No, I don't. I want to stay here," Lizzie answers. Sam tuts.

"Boring," he says.

"That's fine with me," Lizzie speaks getting up.

"Where are you going?" Sam questions.

"I have work," Lizzie answers.

"I'll go with you," Hunter declares getting up, they leave.

At the Joint, Lizzie and Hunter are sitting at the bar making baskets and Taylor is standing behind it.

"What are these for?" Hunter asks.

"There is going to be a party here and they requested handmade baskets," Taylor answers.

"I hate art," Lizzie declares.

"Why am I doing this again?" Hunter questions.

"Because you're here, with nothing to do," Lizzie replies.

"That and the fact that you offered to help," Taylor points out.

"Now I regret it," Hunter responds. Taylor looks at Lizzie and notices she's spaced out.

"What's going on with you?" He asks her.

"Nothing. Just thinking," Lizzie responds.

"About what happened last night?" Hunter queries. Lizzie nods.

"Which part? The Nathan or the Ben part?" Taylor questions.

"Both," Lizzie answers. Erik walks in and everyone looks at him.

"Since you're here. You can help," Lizzie informs him handing him a basket.

"Do I have to?" Erik whines.

"Yes, I'm your favourite," Lizzie responds. Erik grabs the basket and gets to work.

At the Rodriguez, Nathan enters the study room and sits down.

"I know this is poor timing, but we need to plan Raf's funeral," he informs them.

"Of course, did you have anything in mind?" Elliot asks.

"A small get together, for his family. He didn't have many friends," Nathan responds.

"His own fault, I'm sure," Heather says.

"Shouldn't we do this when Erik gets back?" Elliot asks.

"No, he wouldn't really care anyway. Planning things has never been his strong suit," Phoebe tells her.

"Where is he anyway?" Nathan queries.

"At the Joint with Lizzie," Elliot answers. Nathan stops.

"Phoebe can I leave you in charge of planning?" Nathan questions.

"Sure," Phoebe replies. Nathan gets up and leaves.

Back at the Joint, Hunter looks at Lizzie.

"Lizzie, where's your bracelet?" Hunter asks. Lizzie looks at her wrist and realises it has gone.

"I don't know. It must of fell off. It should be here somewhere," Lizzie replies getting up and looking around. Nathan walks in.

"Hi Nathan," Taylor speaks. Lizzie glares at him.

"Hey, Erik. Can you come home, were planning our brother's funeral?" He tells him.

"As fun as that sounds, I'll pass," Erik declares. The door opens and Mandy and Mia come in.

"Hi babe, I didn't realise you would be here," Mia says going over and kissing Nathan.

"I came for my brother," Nathan says.

"Well, you can go. I'm staying here with Lizzie," Erik tells him.

"Wow, seriously. Another one, how many is this now Lizzie? Why do guys fall at your feet, you're not special," Mandy declares.

"Mandy, stop," Mia says. Mandy ignores her.

"I mean if you were that special, Ben wouldn't have gone with me," Mandy continues. Lizzie's eyes turn green. The three boys' notice.

"Lizzie, just ignore her," Hunter starts. Lizzie ignores him and speeds across the room, sending Mandy flying.

"Lizzie!" Erik shouts. Him and Hunter try to run towards her.

"Prohibere," Lizzie mutters. Hunter and Erik's bodies freeze. Nathan pushes Mia across the room. Taylor grabs her and ducks behind the bar with her.

"Well just stay here," he informs her. Lizzie grabs Mandy by the throat and pins her against the wall, she shows her teeth muttering something. Mandy starts panicking. Out of nowhere, Lizzie disappears along with Nathan. Hunter and Erik unfreeze and go to Mandy.

In the clearing in the woods, Lizzie rolls across the floor. She looks up Nathan is standing there with his eyes glowing blue.

"You need to calm down," he says with a raised voice. Lizzie grins while getting up. Eyes still green.

"Like you care, you ignored me all night and all morning," She responds angrily. His eyes go back to normal.

"I'm not perfect Lizzie, and I've never claimed to be. I have a girlfriend," Nathan tells her.

"Trust me, I know," she replies.

At the Joint, the door opens, Ben and Alex come rushing in.

"Where is she?" Alex asks.

"We don't know," Taylor answers.

"Are you okay?" Ben asks going over to Mandy. She goes to answer when blood starts spilling from her mouth.

"What's going on?" Mia questions concerned. Hunter touches her head, he hears three words clearly 'Morietur, Laboriose, Venenum'.

"Die, painfully, poison." He mutters.

"What is that?" Ben asks.

"It's a curse. She's been cursed to die," Hunter answers.

"We need to find Lizzie," Ben demands.

Chapter 14
New Vampire

"We're not leaving here until you calm down," Nathan snaps.

"Fine, then you can stay here," Lizzie says. She looks into his eyes with her green ones.

"Convertat," she mumbles. Nathan falls to the floor; his bones start cracking.

"Lizzie please, this isn't you," he pleads. She just ignores him.

"Enjoy your wolf form because you won't be changing back," Lizzie declares before disappearing. Nathan looks up into the air and howls. Erik, Hunter and Taylor all look out the broken window.

"What is it?" Ben questions.

"Nathan, he's howling. He needs help," Erik answers before getting up and vanishing.

"I'll stay here with the girls and Ben. You guys go," Taylor says to Alex and Hunter. They nod and disappear too.

Erik arrives out in the middle of the woods, he sees Elliot, Heather and Phoebe there.

"Did you hear it to?" He asks them. They nod.

"It was Nathan," Elliot answers looking around. Alex and Hunter arrive.

"It happened here," Hunter informs them leaning down on a darker patch.

"What? What happened here?" Phoebe asks.

"Lizzie, she turned your brother," he answers.

"Why would she do that?" Heather questions.

"Because it wasn't her. Her bodies being taken over by the spirit. She needs to fight it," Hunter responds.

"If she doesn't?" Alex queries.

"She'll be lost forever," Hunter answers.

Back at the Joint, Mandy is coughing into a bucket.

"I'm still really confused. What happened?" Mia asks. Ben looks at Taylor before turning to Mia.

"Go home, you won't remember today ever. You'll believe everything is fine and you had a fun day with your best friend," he compels. Mia nods before leaving.

"What's is going to happen?" Taylor queries.

"She'll die," Lizzie says from the doorway. They both look at her. Ben bares his teeth when Taylor stops him.

"No, you don't want to make her feel threatened. If you do, she'll attack," Taylor warns him. Ben puts his teeth away.

"Lizzie, are you there? Is our Lizzie there?" Ben asks.

"There is no your Lizzie, not anymore," she responds.

"Who am I talking to?" Ben queries.

"Lizzie, just not a version you'll like," Lizzie answers.

"Why are you doing this?" Ben questions as she moves up the room towards the pool table, she picks up a rod.

"Why not? Afterall, none of you have done me any favours. Everybody only wants me when they need a spell, or they need saving. Every time I used my magic for somebody else's needs I got stronger. I had it under control but then some people had to go and make me mad," Lizzie declares throwing the rod across the room.

"Look whatever's happened we can talk about it. Nobody has to die, especially nobody innocent," Ben announces. Lizzie chuckles.

"Innocent. You think she is innocent. I can assure you, she's not," Lizzie informs him, she walks over to Mandy on the chair and kneels in front of her. Mandy looks at her. "You should have stayed in New York, where you belong," Lizzie tells her, she gets up and walks towards the door before stopping and turning around.

"I'd say she has less than an hour left to live. I suggest you use it wisely," Lizzie says before leaving. They both look at Mandy, everyone arrives at the Joint.

"I have a plan," Hunter announces.

"What's the plan?" Alex asks.

"We split up into groups of three. Lizzie and Nathan both have a scent, we follow it, we find them," Hunter answers.

"That's a good idea. I'll take Heather and Erik to go find Nathan," Elliot responds.

"Okay, me, Sam and Hunter. We'll follow Lizzie's scent from the woods," Alex declares.

"So that leaves Phoebe, Vikki and Jake. You follow it from here," Hunter orders.

"What about us?" Taylor questions.

"You guys stay here and watch Mandy," Hunter answers. They all leave, and Taylor rolls his eyes.

"Great, more babysitting," Taylor says sarcastically.

Phoebe, Vikki and Jake are walking through the woods.

"Are you sure we're going the right way?" Vikki asks.

"Yes, me and Jake have her scent. Now we just follow it," Phoebe answers.

"Why are you here again?" Vikki questions Jake.

"Because Phoebe asked," Jake responds. They keep pressing on, Vikki suddenly stops.

"Do you smell that?" She asks. Phoebe sniffs.

"Blood," Phoebe answers. They run in the direction the smell is coming from.

In another part of the woods, Elliot, Heather and Erik wonder around.

"Are you sure he's out here?" Heather checks.

"Yes, his scent is strong," Elliot answers.

"What do we do again?" Erik asks.

"When we find him, we throw this dust over him. It will turn him back a human. Did you bring the spare clothes?" Elliot questions.

"Yeah, they're in the backpack," Erik replies. Suddenly something jumps out a bush, they all spin and see a wolf growling at them.

"Nathan, it's us," Elliot says. He growls louder and walks towards them. Heather steps in front and growls, her eyes turning red. The wolf backs down and she throws dust at it and turns around. Nathan appears, Elliot snatches the backpack and throws it at him.

"Get dressed," he declares. After he is dressed, they all look at Heather.

"You're an alpha?" Erik asks.

"Yes, I got Rafael's powers when I killed him," Heather responds.

"That makes sense, I wondered why I didn't get his powers when he died," Elliot replies.

"What happened with Lizzie?" Erik asks Nathan. He looks at them.

"That was not Lizzie, she was angry. I've never seen her like that," Nathan responds.

"We can't find her. She cursed Mandy; her eyes won't change back from green. Something really must have hurt her," Elliot informs him.

"Not something, someone," Heather responds before walking off. The boys all follow.

Hunter, Alex and Sam are about to give up when Hunter's phone rings, he answers it.

"Phoebe, what's up?" He asks.

"We found blood, it's Lizzie's and there's a lot," Phoebe informs him.

"Have you found her?" He questions.

"No, no sign of Lizzie anywhere," Phoebe says.

"If somethings happened to her, then her vampire side would have kicked in so she could heal. Meaning that her witch side isn't in control, she should be herself," Hunter declares.

"Okay, we'll keep looking. Nathan's been found, he's helping my brothers look," Phoebe tells him before hanging up.

"What's going on?" Sam asks as Hunter puts his phone away.

"They found Lizzie's blood. I don't think we're alone, proceed with caution," Hunter responds as they head off.

Back at the Joint, Mandy is getting worse.

"This is ridiculous, her time is running out," Ben announces.

"You really like her?" Taylor asks.

"Not like that, I only went to the ball with her to make Lizzie jealous. We're not together," Ben answers.

"Then why so concerned?" Taylor queries.

"Because I feel bad, if I didn't use Mandy then Lizzie wouldn't have been hurt and cursed her," Ben explains.

"That's true," Taylor says. Mandy starts hysterically coughing. Taylor looks at the clock.

"Ben, her hours nearly up," Taylor informs him, Ben checks his phone to find no new messages. He looks over at Mandy.

"Then I have no other choice," he says going over to her, he bites his wrist and feeds her the blood.

"Wh-what are you doing?" Taylor asks. Ben looks at him.

"The only thing I can," he replies before snapping her neck. Taylor jumps back looking at her body. Ben notices his expression.

"Don't worry. She'll be fine. I turned her, she'll become a vampire," he assures him.

"What if she doesn't survive?" Taylor questions.

"She will. It's not like a werewolf bite. Anybody can be turned. They just have to survive transition," Ben informs him.

"Which includes what?" Taylor queries.

"When she wakes, she'll be in-between life and death. She will have twenty-four hours to feed. If she does, she becomes a vampire, if she chooses nothing, she will die," Ben explains. Taylor gulps.

After an hour of searching, they give up and head to the house.

"There's nothing, it's like she just disappeared," Vikki says.

"No, she was taken," Heather responds. Deep in the woods, underground Lizzie wakes, and sits up. She hears footsteps approaching and stands. The door opens, she sighs.

"Why am I not surprised," she says looking at him. Rafael stands there.

"I think it's time we had a talk," Rafael replies.

Chapter 15
Missing

"It's been two days and still no trace," Alex says irritated.

"We'll find her," Vikki assures him.

"Will you? The last time Lizzie disappeared we didn't see her for one hundred and sixty-one years," Sam reminds everyone.

"But she left then this time she was taken," Phoebe responds. The front door opens, and Ben comes in with Mandy. Everyone stares.

"Hi," Mandy utters.

"Welcome to the supernatural group," Alex responds.

"You couldn't think of a better name?" Mandy asks.

"Let's get one thing straight. You've been a vampire for one day, that makes you the weakest. Every other vampire in this room in 1000x stronger and faster than you. You'd lose a fight every time," Phoebe warns her.

"That's good to know." Mandy declares.

"Guys come on; I know none of you are happy about this, but she's one of us now. We have to help her," Ben says.

"Why do we have to do anything?" Vikki asks.

"Because if Lizzie didn't curse her, we wouldn't be in this mess," Ben snaps.

"True, but if you didn't use her to make Lizzie jealous, she never would have been cursed," Heather points out.

"So now this is my fault?" Ben asks.

"Exactly, your mess and your fault. You clean it up," Phoebe announces.

"It's not my fault Lizzie was unhinged," Ben responds.

"Oh, but it is," Heather replies.

"How?" He asks.

"She was only like that because of all the hurt and anger building up in her. Hurt and anger you put there when you ditched her at the ball," Vikki answers.

"Guys!" Elliot says, they all ignore him.

"It's not just my fault. What about Nathan?" Ben asks.

"What about me?" Nathan questions.

"You were the one who kept blowing hot and cold. You admit that you're in love with her but then stayed with your girlfriend. You ignored her," Ben points out.

"Hey guys," Hunter announces but nobody pays him any attention.

"All very true facts." Erik says joining in.

"So, in other words it's just you males that messed her up," Vikki declares.

"GUYS!" Hunter declares louder.

"How about this when we get my sister back you both stay away from her. You both stop admitting you have feelings and then ignore her. If any of you really liked my sister, you'd be with her," Alex demands.

"You can't tell us what to do," Ben snaps.

"I just did," Alex replies.

"I'm with him on this, Lizzie needs to focus on her health and none of you guys are helping her with that," Sam responds.

"I was the one who was there for her when none of you were, because you two turned her into something she didn't want to be, and your brother left her chained to a radiator in a fire while you all left. None of you tried finding her and instead her finance got engaged to someone else. So, I don't think any of you can decide what's best for her," Ben declares. Hunter sighs before opening a book and flipping through the pages.

"True, but you did kidnap her. That's how you know each other," Vikki reminds him. All of a suddenly they all grab their heads and fall to the floor. Hunter is standing in Lizzie's area holding his hand up. When he stops, they get up.

"All I'm hearing is that Lizzie, has years of trauma. From all of you. Not one or two, all. And when she sees you all again it only gets worse, not better. Instead of trying to help her you're all standing here playing the blame game, but none of you will admit that you were in the wrong. Honestly, your all being pretty shitty friends right now and this isn't going to help find her," Hunter announces. They all look at each other.

"He's right, I'm sorry," Vikki says.

"Thank you, now while you were all bickering, I was actually doing a spell and I've found where Lizzie is. Are we going to rescue her, or do you want to stay here and argue some more?" Hunter asks.

In the tunnels, Rafael enters the room Lizzie is in.

"It's been two days; you can't keep ignoring me," Rafael says.

"Why aren't I healing?" Lizzie asks.

"I don't know, but it's a good thing, the longer you take to heal, the longer your witch side stays inactive and I'd rather talk to sane Lizzie then mental Lizzie," Rafael answers. She glares at him.

"What do you want?" She questions.

"To go home," he replies.

"Then go, I don't care," Lizzie responds.

"I need your help," Rafael tells her.

"You, want, my, help? Seriously, why would I ever help you? You've tried to kill me, multiple times. You hate me," Lizzie reminds him.

"I don't hate you," Rafael says.

"You have a funny way of showing it," Lizzie responds. They stand there in silence.

"What did I ever do to you?" She asks. He sighs.

"You came along, and I lost my family. They put you first all the time. Remember that hostage situation in Budapest, they had to choose between me and you. They could only save one and they chose you! Over their own flesh and blood," Rafael answers.

"I'm sorry, I really am. But that wasn't my fault. They made that choice, not me. Plus, it happened a hundred years ago, you need to let it go," Lizzie says. They hear a noise in the tunnels.

"What's that?" Lizzie asks. Rafael listens.

"Hunters. We need to go," he answers.

"I'm not going anywhere with you," Lizzie says.

"Fine, then go your own way. Just think about what I said," he tells her before disappearing. Lizzie sighs and follows. The door opens and Alex enters with Hunter.

"She's not here," Alex declares.

"She was," Hunter responds. Alex looks at him.

"How do you know?" He asks. Hunter points at the floor.

"Blood and it's fresh. She's not long left and she wasn't alone; I'm picking up another scent," Hunter replies. Nathan enters the room.

"It's empty down here. No trace of anyone," he informs them, he goes to leave but stops.

"What is it?" Alex asks.

"I know that scent," he answers.

"You do? How?" Hunter questions.

"I'm not sure, but it feels familiar," he says before leaving.

In the woods, Rafael and Lizzie are walking.

"I knew you'd come with me," he announces.

"I didn't do it for you, I did it for survival. I'm injured and I'm not healing properly, and like you pointed out my witch side isn't working. The best chance I have at staying alive is with you," Lizzie declares.

"That's true, but how do you know I won't leave at the first sign of trouble?" Rafael asks.

"Because like you said, you need me. Plus, we can make a deal. You get me home safely; I'll convince your family to let you stay," Lizzie informs him. Rafael looks at her a minute.

"Okay, you have a deal," he says before heading off, she follows.

They arrive at her house and go inside.

"Hello?" Lizzie shouts, no answers.

"Guess no one's home," she says. Rafael walks over to her area and picks up something from the table.

"I think they found your bracelet," he announces, she walks over.

"May I?" He asks, Lizzie holds her wrist out and he puts it on. He then grabs a glass, bites his wrist and puts his blood in the glass and hands it to her. She looks at him.

"My blood will heal you ten times faster and now you have your bracelet, I don't have to worry about you attacking me," he informs her, she takes it and drinks it. The injury on her leg vanishes. Just then the front door opens, and everyone walks in, they stop when they see Lizzie and Rafael. Everyone looks at each other.

"You were dead," Alex says.

"And yet, here I am," Rafael responds.

"You kidnapped Lizzie?" Erik asks.

"Saved, the hunters attacked her," Rafael answers.

"He brought me home too," Lizzie informs them.

"It's been two days," Sam tells her.

"I know," Lizzie says.

"Hang on a minute. Let's rewind. How are you alive? Heather ripped your heart out," Vikki reminds him.

"A protection spell, he got Leah to put one on him before the battle," Lizzie explains.

"So, you died, and then came back?" Phoebe asks. Rafael nods.

"Why didn't you come home?" Elliot questions.

"I wasn't sure how you would react, so I went into hiding," Rafael answers.

"We would have been happy that you weren't dead," Phoebe points out.

"If your still alive, how is Heather an alpha?" Nathan asks.

"Because he did die, once she killed him, she got his powers. He came back, but not as an alpha. Just as a werewolf," Lizzie speaks. Rafael looks at Heather.

"You must be happy with your new power," he says. Heather glares at him. The door opens and Ben walks through with Mandy. He stops when he sees Rafael.

"You're supposed to be dead," Ben announces.

"Funny, I was about to say the same thing about her," Lizzie responds. Ben looks at Mandy and then back at Lizzie.

"There is a reasonable explanation to all of this," Ben informs her. Lizzie looks at Rafael.

"Welcome home," she says before leaving the room, followed by Ben.

They enter Bens room.

"How is she alive?" Lizzie asks.

"I turned her," Ben answers. She looks at him.

"Are you out of your mind? You turned her into a vampire," she retorts.

"Well, what was I supposed to do? You hexed her; I didn't want to believe that you actually wanted her dead. Time was running out, so I made a decision. It might not have been the best one, but I made it. I wasn't going to let her die and I know that you never would of forgave yourself if she did," Ben explains. Lizzie looks at him.

"You're right. I didn't want her dead, but I did want her to suffer and a part of me wanted you to suffer too," Lizzie replies.

"I know, what I did was wrong. I should not have left you alone like that. I'm sorry," he answers.

"It doesn't matter now. You turned her, she's your responsibility," Lizzie informs him before leaving.

Chapter 16
The Island of Wonder

At the Rodriguez, they all sit around the table in silence.

"Well, this is awkward," Erik points out. Phoebe kicks him.

"I would just like to say that I'm sorry for the pain I've caused. I will do better," Rafael informs them.

"And my son? Are you still a danger to him?" Heather questions.

"Of course, not. Your son is perfectly safe," he assures her.

"I doubt it," Heather answers before getting up and leaving.

"Something I said?" Rafael asks innocently. Erik and Nathan just glare at him.

A few days later, Lizzie is sitting on the sofa reading a book, she hears a scratching noise coming from down in the basement. Alex comes down the stairs.

"Me and Vikki are going out. Sam is with Evie and Ben is training Mandy out in the back. Will you be, okay?" He asks. Lizzie looks at him.

"Yeah, I have a book," she responds waving it at him.

"That's not what I meant," he replies.

"I know, I'll be fine. Don't worry about me," she informs him as Vikki comes down the stairs, they leave. Once the door is closes Lizzie hears the scratching again. She gets up putting the book down and goes down the stairs. She walks over to the basement door; the scratching is louder inside. She grabs the handle, takes a deep breath and pushes the door open. In the corner of the room is a figure, Lizzie steps in and the figure stands and emerges. She sees Tyron, he has chains around his hands.

"Elizabeth, I wondered how long it would be until you paid me a visit," he declares. Lizzie sprints across the room and grabs him by the throat.

"Give me one reason why I shouldn't rip your throat out," Lizzie announces.

"Because I know how to help," he responds in breathes, as his throat is being crushed. Lizzie looks at him and then drops him to the floor.

"Help? With what? You were the threat and now you're locked up," she reminds him.

"True I might be locked up in here but I'm not the only threat this world will face. There will be more battles to face, but right now you're fighting the biggest battle. Yourself," Tyron informs her. She looks at him.

"What are you talking about?" She asks.

"The spirit that's taking over your witch side. Oh yes, I know all about it. I also know that the bracelet won't be able to contain it forever, it will take over. Unless of course, you stop it," Tyron answers.

"And let me guess, you know exactly what I need to do that?" Lizzie questions.

"Indeed, I do," he replies. She shakes her head.

"I'm not buying it; you will say anything to get out this cell," Lizzie tells him turning around and walking towards the door.

"You're right, I will say anything. But in this case, I am speaking the truth," he says. She stops and looks at him.

"And why would you help me?" Lizzie queries.

"Because I meant what I said. I want the world to be a better place, but there won't be a world to change if you can't be stopped. All that power could be the end, for everyone," Tyron explains. She studies him for a minute.

"So, how do I stop it?" She asks.

"You have to go on a journey to the island where it all began, but you can't go alone. You need all three alphas if you wish to destroy the spirit," Tyron informs her. She walks out the room, closing the door behind her.

She heads into her bedroom and messages Taylor.

Lizzie: **Hey, Taylor. I need you to come to mine right away. Bring your dad.**

Taylor: **Why? Is everything okay?**

Lizzie: **I'll explain when you get here.**

She messages Heather too and then heads down the stairs, going over to her workspace she starts working on a spell. Taylor, Michael, Heather and Hunter all arrive at hers.

"What's the emergency?" Heather asks. Lizzie looks at them all.

"I need your help. There may be a way to get rid of the spirit that's linked to my magic," Lizzie says.

"How? I've looked through all spell books, I found nothing," Hunter responds.

"There's an island, I'll find the answer there," Lizzie replies.

"How do you know this?" Hunter asks. His father enters the room.

"I told her," he says. They all turn to look at him.

"No, no way. You're going to trust him, after everything he's done," Heather declares.

"No, I don't trust him. But what if he is right, even after spending weeks in our basement his goal has not changed. He still wants supernatural's extinct and right now I'm the biggest threat the world faces," Lizzie announces.

"I don't like it," Hunter says.

"I know, that's why we're not going alone. I need the three alphas for the spell, and a witch to perform it," Lizzie tells him. Hunter looks at her.

"What if he turns against us or tries to hurt one of us?" He questions.

"He can't," Lizzie answers. Tyron holds up his wrist where there is a black bracelet.

"I enchanted it, he can't take it off and it weakens his power, making him less of a threat," Lizzie explains. She looks at them all.

"Are you in?" She asks.

An hour later, there is a minibus outside. Hunter and Taylor are loading on their bags.

"My dad should be back by now," Taylor says. Lizzie looks at him.

"They'll be here," she responds. Heather walks over followed by Rafael.

"Why is he coming again?" He asks Lizzie.

"Because Tyron is sneaky and dangerous, and I don't trust him. If anyone can tell when somebody has an ulterior motive, it's Rafael," Lizzie answers.

"Plus, I want to prove that I am changing into a better person. What better way to do that then helping the girl who everyone adores?" Rafael queries. Lizzie looks at him.

"Get on the bus," she demands, he does. Michael and Tyron arrive.

"Did you get it?" Hunter asks. Tyron grins and pulls a skull out his bag.

"What is that?" Lizzie asks.

"A skull," Tyron replies.

"I know that, who's?" She queries.

"Oh, that's not important," he answers.

"Clearly it is if you had to break into a museum to get it," Lizzie reminds him. He just shrugs and gets in the passenger side.

"Who's driving again?" Hunter asks.

"I am. It was meant to be Tyron but I'm positive he'll drive us off a cliff. Your dad is one journey away from crazy town," Michael informs Hunter before getting in the driver's side. Taylor and Heather get in the back as a car pulls up.

"Oh great, this should be fun," Lizzie says to Hunter. Alex gets out of the driver's side. Sam and Vikki following. He looks at the minibus.

"You can't be serious? You're actually going to do this?" He asks.

"I have no other choice. It could be the only way to save everyone," Lizzie responds.

"But Tyron, really? That man is insane. What if you get there and it was all a lie?" Alex questions.

"Then he won't make it off the island," Lizzie answers. Alex looks at her.

"Lizzie please, two of these people have tried to kill you. The only person I trust to keep you safe is Taylor, and he's new to the whole being a werewolf thing," he responds.

"Seriously? I've helped save your sisters life and keep her safe and you don't trust me," Hunter declares.

"Not really, no," Alex replies. Hunter sighs and gets on the bus.

"Then come with us and if Tyron does anything wrong you can kill him yourself," Lizzie informs him.

"I will," Alex says heading inside. He comes out a few minutes later with a bag and heads to the trailer at the back. Vikki goes over to him.

"You're actually going to go?" She asks.

"Of course, Lizzie's my sister," Alex answers.

"I know, but she's also capable of looking out for herself," Vikki points out.

"I've just got her back. There's no way I'm letting her go off without my help," Alex announces. Lizzie and Sam are standing next to the minibus doors. Alex and Vikki walk over.

"Be careful," Sam says to Lizzie.

"I always am," Lizzie replies, she goes and hugs Vikki.

"Why is it every time I get you back in my life you're going off on a crazy journey?" Vikki asks. Lizzie looks at her and smiles.

"The next crazy journey can be ours," she tells her before getting on the bus with Alex. The door closes and they pull off.

Phoebe, Erik and Nathan arrive home and go to the study room Elliot is sitting on the sofa reading a book.

"Where's Raf and Heather?" Phoebe asks.

"Gone," Elliot answers.

"What together? That's unexpected," Erik responds. Elliot looks at him.

"Not like that, they've gone with Lizzie to an island that will help with the spirit," Elliot tells him.

"Wait what?" Nathan asks. Elliot sighs and puts the book down.

"It's a long story but Tyron told Lizzie he knows how to help her; so now Lizzie, Tyron, Heather, Rafael, Michael and Hunter have gone on a journey to some island," Elliot explains.

"Why weren't we told?" Phoebe asks. Elliot shrugs.

"How should I know?" He questions picking up the book again. Nathan throws himself on the sofa opposite, while Phoebe and Erik go upstairs.

After a few hours, Lizzie and the rest get off a boat on an island.

"Welcome to Island of wonder," Tyron announces. Everyone looks at each other.

"Let's not forget why we're here," Alex reminds them.

"Of course not, I brought some tents because it will take longer than a day to find the place," Tyron informs them holding up four tent bags.

"What are we even looking for?" Heather asks.

"A cave, it will probably be on the far side of the island considering that's where all the rocks are, this side is just water and jungle," Tyron answers.

"So how do we get there?" Michael questions.

"Through the jungle," Tyron responds walking off towards it, everyone reluctantly follows. After a while, Taylor holds up his phone.

"There's no signal," he tells everyone.

"Well duh, you're on an island in the middle of nowhere. What did you expect?" Tyron asks. They wonder around for a few hours before it starts getting dark. They find a nice clear space and set up camp. Michael and Tyron are arguing over the tent.

"I know how to put a tent up," Tyron tells him.

"So, do I. It's bad enough I have to share with you, you don't need to tell me what to do," Michael responds. Lizzie looks across at them and waves her hand, the tent puts itself up. They both look at her.

"You're welcome," she says going and sitting around the campfire. They join.

"So, I have a question," Hunter declares.

"What's the question?" Lizzie asks.

"Dad, how did you know about this place and the head?" He questions. Tyron just shrugs.

"No, I'm with Hunter. We agreed to come out here blindly, you could at least tell us what you know," Heather says. Tyron sighs.

"Fine. It was three hundred years ago, legend has it that the first ever wolf packs were created then. Three brave leaders united their packs and decided to live in harmony. Abe was the leader of the moonshine pack; Ambrose was the leader of the twilight and Daphne was the leader of the shadow pack. They initiated three people, turned them into wolves to make their packs stronger. Ambrose was careless he turned anyone and everyone, the legend says that he turned a girl, only seventeen. This girl was no ordinary girl, her name was Keres. Which in Greek stands for evil spirit. She was a witch, and he knew."

"He wanted to use her as a weapon against the other two packs, he wanted the island to himself. She started causing problems for the packs, making them turn against each other. When Abe and Daphne found out what she was, they were furious at Ambrose, he had gone against the laws of nature. They made a deal; they perform a ritual to bound her witch side and Abe and Daphne would take there's packs and leave the island. They were all in agreement. The day of the ritual came, and Keres was tied onto a bonfire, each alpha gave their blood, and her witch side was removed. When she died, her body was buried and her head was removed, now her spirit lives on looking for new life," Tyron explains.

"That sounds like a load of crap," Rafael says.

"Believe what you want, you asked for the story," Tyron replies.

"So, the head you're carrying around is the head of a seventeen-year-old girl?" Taylor asks. Tyron nods.

"On that note, I'm going to bed. Goodnight, everyone," Lizzie announces getting up and heading into a tent.

Chapter 17
The Legend

Back at Greenwich the next day Phoebe enters the joint and sees Jake behind the bar and Vikki sitting there slurping a milkshake. She goes over.

"Hey Jake, how come you're working here?" She asks.

"I'm looking after the place for Michael, him and Taylor went with Lizzie yesterday," Jake answers.

"Taylor got to go?" Phoebe questions.

"And Alex," Vikki says. Phoebe looks at her. Jake notices.

"Hey, it's no big deal. You can hang with me here," he tells her. Phoebe looks at him.

"Thanks babe, but they've all gone on an adventure and we weren't even invited," she responds. Just then Evie rushes in and goes over to them.

"Where's Lizzie?" She asks.

"Not here, why?" Vikki questions.

"You guys remember my friend Brooke?" Evie queries.

"Vaguely," Phoebe answers. Evie looks around the room and then at the girls.

"Well spit it out," Vikki tells her. She grabs Phoebe's arm and runs towards the door, Vikki sighs before getting up and following. Once outside Evie takes them into the alleyway where Brooke is standing.

"What is this?" Vikki asks. Evie and Brooke look at each other before pushing a bin out the way, on the floor is a dead body.

"What happened?" Phoebe asks.

"It was an accident. He started attacking us," Brooke answers really fast.

"Evie?" Vikki questions looking at her.

"It was Brooke, he had a knife, and he was trying to mug us. Brooke went to push him away and he flew, the knife stabbed him," Evie explains. Phoebe and Vikki look at Brooke.

"You're a witch?" Phoebe asks.

"I don't think so, I've done anything like that before," Brooke answers.

"Okay Brooke, who do you live with?" Vikki questions.

"My mum," Brooke responds.

"Is she home now?" Phoebe asks. Brooke nods.

"Well then, lets pay her a visit," Vikki says, they all head off.

Sometime later they arrive at a mansion.

"You live here?" Phoebe asks.

"Yeah, my mum's the mayor," Brooke answers, they walk towards the door. Brooke opens it and her and Evie go inside, Phoebe and Vikki can't.

"Brooke is that you?" Her mum shouts heading down the stairs.

"Yeah, I brought some friends back is that okay?" Brooke asks.

"Of course, come on in. We don't bite," Her mum says. Vikki and Phoebe enter, and they all go to the living room.

"So, what are you ladies up to today?" Mayor Campbell asks.

"Actually, we came to talk to you," Evie answers.

"Is everything okay?" She asks.

"How long have you known that you're a witch?" Phoebe questions. Everyone looks at her.

"I beg your pardon?" Mayor Campbell asks.

"Apologise for her. What she meant was we know that you're a witch because Brooke discovered she's one today," Vikki answers. Mayor Campbell looks at Brooke.

"Is this true?" She queries. Brooke nods and sits down with her mum and Evie does the same.

"I'm sorry I never told you before, I was waiting for something like this first," Her mum says.

"It's fine Mum, I'm just glad I know now," Brooke replies. Mayor Campbell looks at Phoebe and Vikki.

"How do you know about witches?" She asks them.

"We know all about the supernatural world. I'm a vampire and Phoebe is half vampire, half wolf," Vikki answers.

"Evie was meant to get Lizzie, what happened?" Brooke questions.

"Lizzie wasn't with them," Evie replies.

"What does Lizzie have to do with this?" The mayor queries.

"Lizzie is half witch, half vampire," Vikki responds.

"Where is Lizzie anyway?" Brooke asks.

"She went to this island thing to get rid of some spirit taken over her body," Phoebe answers.

"Keres," The mayor says.

"What?" Evie asks.

"It's an old legend. Lizzie must be crazy to agree to that," Mayor Campbell answers.

"Why it's a good thing. She's only getting rid of the spirit," Phoebe tells her.

"It doesn't work like that. In the story when the wolves tried to bound Keres witch side, it went wrong. The witch that performed the magic changed the spell, instead she bound the wolf side. That only made Keres stronger, the only way to stop her was for the alphas to combine their blood and trap her, once they did that, they then used a knife made out of lobelia to kill her. Once she was dead, they removed her head," Mayor Campbell tells them.

"What happened to her head?" Vikki questions.

"It was kept in a safe place, apparently whoever has the head can find their way to the cave where the first ritual was performed and the rest of the body lays. Once the head is returned to the body and the spell is done, Keres will be reborn. Whoever's body she took host in will no longer live," Mayor Campbell explains. Phoebe and Vikki look at each other before running out the house.

Phoebe runs into the study room all three of her brothers look at her.

"We need to go," she tells them.

"Where?" Erik asks.

"To Lizzie, it's all a trick. He's going to kill her," Phoebe responds.

"How do you know this?" Elliot asks.

"I'll explain on the way, come on. Vikki is meeting us at the docks with Sam," Phoebe answers. Her brothers get up and follow her out the house.

On the Island of wonders, everyone is hiking through the jungle. Lizzie is walking next to Taylor, he stops.

"Is everything okay?" Lizzie asks him. He waits until everyone else is out of earshot.

"No, Lizzie I woke up last night to use the toilet and I overheard Tyron," He responds.

"Overheard him saying what?" Lizzie queries. He holds out a piece of paper.

"This, it's Latin so I don't understand it, but I thought you might," Taylor replies.

"How did you get this?" She questions. He just looks at her.

"Never mind," she says opening it up. She starts reading, halfway though she pauses and looks at Taylor.

"What? What is it?" He asks.

"It's a spell," she responds.

"What sort of spell?" He queries.

"The sort of spell that makes you trade places with a dead person," Lizzie declares before storming off after everyone else. Taylor runs after her.

"Let's stop here," Tyron says to the group as they reach the top of the hill. There's a waterfall and a river just below them.

"The waterfall is pretty," Heather announces.

"It's been here for years," Tyron tells her. Just then he goes flying into the water, Lizzie appears on the edge. Everyone gathers round.

"What the hell is wrong with you?" Tyron shouts up.

"You know I really wanted to believe that you would help, I wanted to believe that there was some good in you. I guess

I was wrong. I know about the spell; you were going to trade my life for some dead girl," Lizzie exclaims.

"How do you even know about that?" He asks. She holds up the paper.

"It was given to me; I should have listened to everyone who warned me about you," Lizzie responds before turning and walking away, everyone slowly follows.

At the docks, Phoebe and her brothers meet up with Vikki, Sam and Ben.

"Are we really doing this?" Phoebe asks Vikki.

"Yes, it's the only way to warn them," Vikki answers.

"That is if we're not too late," Erik points out, they all stare at him. Just then a car pulls up behind them. Jake, Brooke and Evie get out.

"No, you're not coming with us," Sam says.

"We don't want too," Evie responds.

"Then why are you here?" Erik asks.

"My mum, she told me how to help Lizzie," Brooke answers.

"How?" Phoebe questions.

"The spirit Keres, she only picks host who have a lot of negative emotions. Hurt, anger anything like that. If you want to get rid of Keres, then Lizzie needs to let it out, she needs to let her emotions out," Brooke informs them.

"How the hell is she supposed to do that?" Sam asks.

"I know how," Vikki answers, she runs towards the nearest boat.

"Tell your mum we said thank you, we'll see you when we get back," Phoebe yells as they follow. They all pile into the boat and leave.

"Do we even know where to go?" Elliot queries.

"It can't be too hard; we need to look for an island that will already have a boat," Vikki responds.

"There might be few islands that look like that," Erik points out.

"That's okay, there's seven of us. If we need to, we can split up," Vikki says.

"Or one of us could you know, howl. It's just a thought though," Nathan declares.

"That could work too," Vikki replies.

Everyone is walking through the island.

"Lizzie, slow down," Heather shouts as they try to keep up with her.

"Lizzie!" Hunter exclaims grabbing her. She stops and realises that she's on the edge off a cliff. They turn around as everyone approaches.

"Are you okay?" Alex asks her. She nods. Hunter, Taylor, Michael, Heather and Rafael look up.

"What, what's wrong?" Lizzie asks.

"Nathan, I can hear him howling," Rafael answers.

"How? We're miles away in the middle of nowhere," Lizzie responds. Rafael looks at her.

"I don't know," he says before howling back.

On the boat in the middle of the sea, Nathan goes to howl again and then stops.

"That way, I heard Rafael from over there," he informs them. Elliot and Sam row faster. Eventually they approach an island.

"This has to be it," Elliot says getting out the boat and pushing it to shore, everyone gets out.

"We should split up. Me, Erik and Nathan will go one way, you four go the other way," Elliot demands before walking off. Ben, Sam, Vikki and Phoebe look at each other before going the other way.

At the cliff, everyone is looking around.

"Who remembers which way we came?" Heather asks.

"I do," Tyron answers appearing behind Rafael and snapping his neck.

Chapter 18
Spirit of Keres

Everyone turns to face him. Hunter looks at his wrist.

"His bracelet, where is it?" He asks.

"Oh that, it wasn't waterproof, so when Elizabeth threw me in, the magic wore off," Tyron answers.

"Lizzie, run," Alex demands. Lizzie looks at him before grabbing Taylor's hand and running off. They run for a while before Taylor stops. Lizzie looks at him.

"What? Why did you stop?" Lizzie questions.

"Because you'll be faster by yourself," Taylor replies.

"No, I am not leaving you," Lizzie declares. Taylor looks around.

"Over there, there's a cave. Let's just hide out in there, he'll give up eventually," Taylor says. Lizzie nods and they run towards the cave.

Vikki, Sam, Phoebe and Ben all head up the cliff side.

"Guys!" Sam shouts running towards the bodies. He goes over to Alex. Rafael is sitting next to Heather.

"Raf, what happened?" Phoebe asks.

"Tyron, he did this. Lizzie found out that it was all a trick and confronted him. We escaped but then he found us again," Rafael answers.

"Where is Lizzie now?" Sam asks.

"I don't know. He took me out first," Rafael says. Vikki and Ben go over to Michaels body that is slumped on the floor, blood everywhere. Sam reaches into his bag and pulls out a bottle of water, he opens it and chucks it over Alex who jolts up. He looks up.

"Sam," he says relieved. Sam helps him up off the floor as Heather comes around.

"He took Hunter," Heather tells them.

"What?" Vikki asks.

"Tyron. He stabbed Hunter and took him," she says.

"What about Lizzie?" Sam asks.

"I told her to run, she took Taylor with her," Alex explains. Michael grunts as he sits up.

"He stabbed me and then he stole my blood, Heather's too," He informs them. Vikki and Ben help him up.

"Let's find them," Phoebe says. She howls. On the other side of the jungle, Elliot, Erik and Nathan stop running.

"Phoebe," Elliot speaks. He looks at his brothers and they take off in that direction.

Lizzie and Taylor arrive in the cave, Taylor looks back towards the entrance as Lizzie stops.

"Taylor, it's that cave," she declares. Taylor turns around and looks in the middle of the room where there is a skeleton lying on a stone table. The skeleton has no head. They look at each other.

"Let's get out of here," Taylor says, they turn around and see Tyron.

"Elizabeth, how lovely it is to find you here," Tyron speaks, he is dragging Hunter's body. He chucks it on the floor and Hunter sits up, blood pouring from his stomach.

"What did you do to him?" Lizzie asks. Tyron looks at his son.

"Just sedated him with wolfsbane. He can't go anywhere, but he can still do my spell," Tyron answers. Taylor pulls Lizzie back.

"You don't have to do this," Taylor tells him.

"I do, it's the only way. I bring her back and then I kill her. Once she is dead every other witch should slowly follow. One problem solved," Tyron explains. He walks over towards the stone table and places the skull above the rest of the body, Lizzie looks at Hunter knelt on the floor. He pulls a small knife out of his pocket and looks at Lizzie. Tyron takes a step back and Hunter stabs him in the back of the leg.

"Go Lizzie, run," Hunter shouts, Lizzie looks at Taylor who nods. She runs past Hunter and Tyron and out of the cave. Tyron yells and gets up and follows. Once Lizzie is outside, she runs straight towards the jungle edge.

"Elizabeth!" Tyron shouts, she stops and turns to face him. He is standing opposite her near the cave entrance and she is standing near the jungle entrance. They stand there looking at each other. Everyone runs out of the jungle behind Lizzie, she looks behind her at all of them.

"I won't stop, if you don't come with me now, I will go back into that cave and I'll kill your friends and I won't stop," Tyron warns her. Sam takes a step towards Lizzie.

"Lizzie, you don't need him to get rid of it. You can do it, just let it out. Stop holding onto all that pain, all that hurt. Let it go," Sam tells her holding out his hand, Lizzie looks at him and then down at her bracelet. She looks back at Tyron before unclipping her bracelet.

"NO!" Tyron shouts, he starts running towards Lizzie. She hands her bracelet to Sam and then looks across at where Tyron is running. She closes her eyes, takes a deep breath and screams. The scream knocks Tyron of his feet and sends him flying back towards the cave, he smashes into the side of it. The floor starts shaking, Lizzie stops and falls into Alex's arm. They look down towards the cave that starts to shake.

"The cave, it's collapsing," Sam says.

"No," Lizzie responds, Alex helps her up and she runs towards it.

"Lizzie!" Alex shouts running after her with Sam.

Inside the cave Taylor tries to help Hunter off the floor, they hear the cave shake.

"What's happening?" Taylor asks.

"The cave, it's collapsing," Hunter replies. A rock falls in front of the entrance.

"Oh God, I'm going to die," Taylor declares as the rest of the rocks start collapsing too. Hunter looks up and sees one shaking above Taylors head, he looks at Taylor and then tackles him to the floor.

Outside Lizzie stops running as the rest of the cave collapses.

"NOO!" She screams. Alex and Sam catch up with her, everyone else following at bay. Michael falls to his knees.

"Taylor," He says defeated, tears forming in his eyes. Some of the rocks start to move.

"There!" Heather speaks, they all look over in the direction, a rock hits the floor and underneath is a shield. Hunter is lying on top of Taylor, a protective shield around them. Taylor looks up into Hunters eyes as the shield comes down. Hunter hurriedly gets up from on top of him and helps him up. They look around in the open, Lizzie looks relieved and then runs towards them. Taylor looks at Hunter.

"Thank you, for saving me," he says.

"It was nothing," Hunter tells him. Lizzie arrives and throws herself around Taylor, he hugs her back.

"I thought you were dead," Lizzie declares.

"I'm fine," Taylor responds. Lizzie lets go off him as everyone else approaches. Michael goes over to Taylor and puts his arms on his shoulders, he looks at him for a minute before hugging him. Lizzie looks at Hunter.

"What?" He asks.

"I knew you cared," she answers.

"I don't know what you're talking about," he replies. Lizzie walks away from him as Ben approaches. Hunter and Ben look at each other for a minute.

"I'm glad you're okay," Ben says.

"Thanks, you too," Hunter responds. Ben nods before walking off.

"Come on guys. Let's go home," Vikki declares. They all head off together.

A few days later, Lizzie is walking the school corridor, she approaches Brooke.

"Hey, can I ask you something?" She asks.

"Sure," Brooke answers.

"How did your mum know what to do?" She questions.

"I don't know, she just told me to pass the message on. She did tell me to tell you that, a part of Keres is always going to be connected to you and your dark side. When she's not able to control you anymore, your eyes will still turn green and that you need to be careful and stay away from stress," Brooke informs her. Lizzie nods.

"Thanks, I actually came to give you this," She replies handing out a book. Brooke takes it.

"What is it?" She asks.

"A spell book, I used it when I first became a witch. Evie mentioned that your mum hasn't got any time to help you. If you'd like, I'd be happy to show you," Lizzie tells her. Brooke takes the book.

"Thanks Lizzie," She says closing her locker. They head off down the corridor together. After school, Lizzie arrives home, she looks at Sam on the sofa.

"Why didn't you come school today?" She asks.

"I've decided not to go back. I'm twenty-seven and school is boring," he answers picking up a leaflet.

"I'd rather plan my holiday," he informs her.

"When are you going again?" She questions sitting next to him.

"In about six weeks when the summer starts," he replies.

"Where is everyone else?" She queries.

"Hunter is at the joint, Vikki is in the bath, Alex is shopping, and Ben is out with Mandy again. He's really struggling to help her," he responds. He looks at her.

"You could always help him; you know build on your friendship, which is falling apart," he points out.

"You know I could, but I'm supposed to be staying away from stress and Mandy is the biggest stress I know," Lizzie exclaims.

"Okay, or maybe this has something to do with you not facing your feelings. You haven't spoken to Ben and Nathan since we got back, five days ago and you know they both came all the way to an island just to save your life. You can't ignore them forever," he informs her.

At the joint, Hunter is sitting on a far table, Taylor walks over.

"Hey, you've been here an hour and haven't ordered anything. Is there anything I can help you with?" He asks. Hunter looks at him.

"No, I'm good," he answers. Taylor sighs and sits opposite him.

"Why are you here then?" He questions.

"I was just making sure you were okay; you know you mean a lot to Lizzie and I care about her," Hunter responds awkwardly getting up. "I'll tell her that you're okay," He says walking backwards and bumping into a table. He turns and runs into Lizzie. He looks at her before hurrying out the door, Lizzie smiles and looks at Taylor.

At the clearing in the middle of the woods is Ben and Mandy. Ben is trying to teach Mandy how to adjust to being a vampire.

"So, what do you do when you get hungry?" He asks.

"I look for a prey and I attack," Mandy answers.

"And then?" He questions.

"Nothing, they're dead," Mandy says.

"No, that's not what you do. You don't feed to the point where they die. You feed a little and then you compel them to forget. We've been over this now a few times," Ben reminds her.

"But why compel them to forget when you could just kill them?" Mandy queries.

"Because you don't want to kill someone. Trust me, it's not a nice feeling," Ben informs her. Mandy just shrugs.

"Okay, let's try something else. I'll show you how to fight, run at me," Ben says. Mandy looks at him before running, as she approaches Ben puts his arm out and she tumbles over it.

"Now try again but be on guard. Check your surroundings, use your hearing and speed. If you win, I'll buy you a shake," Ben tells her. She gets up off the floor and tries again. After a few more tries and Mandy being chucked on the floor, she succeeds. She runs towards him and slides under his arm and takes his leg out. He tumbles on the floor next to her. Ben sits up.

"Well done, that was really unexpected," He praises.

"I learnt from the best," she tells him. He chuckles and looks next to him where Mandy is sitting. She catches his eye and leans in to kiss him. He pulls back.

"I can't, I'm sorry," he says. She looks at him.

"No, I get it. You're in love with Lizzie," she replies.

"I never meant to use you," Ben tells her.

"How long have you been in love with her?" Mandy asks.

"For forty years," Ben answer.

"Then go and get her, stop wasting time," Mandy declares. Ben gets up off the floor and helps Mandy up.

"Thank you," he says before disappearing.

Lizzie and Taylor are sitting on a table at the joint.

"Do you think Tyron will come back?" Taylor asks.

"Probably, he has some serious issues," Lizzie answers.

"What about you?" Taylor questions.

"What about me?" Lizzie asks.

"What are you going to do if he does come back?" Taylor queries.

"Honestly, I don't want to think about it. I just want try and get through the rest of the school year without any more problems," Lizzie replies. Taylor takes her hand.

"You know, you showed me what you all were and everything, but you never told me how old anyone really is. Can I know?" He asks. Lizzie smiles at him.

"I'm twenty-five. Sam is twenty-seven. Alex is twenty-nine. Vikki is twenty-eight and Ben is twenty-six," Lizzie says.

"What about the other family. How old is Nathan?" Taylor queries.

"Nathan is twenty-eight and Elliot is thirty-one," Lizzie informs him.

"I'm twenty-six," Erik declares going over. They both look at him.

"Are you the youngest?" Taylor asks.

"No Phoebe is, she's twenty-four," Erik declares. Taylor looks at Lizzie.

"Okay, so you're twenty-five and you're failing school. Why don't you just drop out, your brother did," he says.

"I'm not a quitter," Lizzie responds.

"If that was true, you wouldn't have quit on Nathan and Ben," Erik exclaims. Lizzie stands up and looks at him.

"I didn't quit on them, they picked someone else. There's a difference," She replies before leaving.

She arrives home that night and goes into her bedroom, Ben is waiting for her.

"Ben, what are you doing?" She asks.

"We need to talk," He answers.

"About what?" She questions.

"Us," He replies.

"Ben, there isn't an us," Lizzie informs him.

"I want there to be, you said you liked me too, but it wasn't the right time to be together. I've been thinking about it and there's never going to be a right time, so why can't we be together?" Ben queries. Lizzie looks at him and then goes over and kisses him.

"We can be together," she tells him. He kisses her back and picks her up.

Chapter 19
Celebrate

It has been a few weeks, and before anyone knows it's time for graduation.

"Can you believe we've survived this year. No more Mandy after today, she's going back to New York," Evie says to Brooke. Lizzie and Erik look at them.

"You don't know?" Erik asks.

"Know what?" Brooke queries.

"Mandy isn't going back to New York, she's staying here," he answers.

"Why?" Evie queries.

"Because she's a vampire," Lizzie tells them. Evie and Brooke look at each other.

"Are you serious, since when? Why did no one tell us?" Brooke exclaims.

"Honestly, I've decided to start ignoring my problems until they go away or die," Lizzie informs them.

"I didn't think it was important," Erik says.

"I just don't care what Mandy does," Taylor points out.

"I heard my name!" Mandy declares. Lizzie rolls her eyes.

"Maybe because we were talking about you," Lizzie says.

"Well, that's just rude," Mandy replies. Lizzie looks at her.

"Does it look like I care?" She asks before walking away. Taylor and Erik grin before following. They head inside to get their robes.

"Hey guys, what's going on?" Jake asks approaching them in his robe, Lizzie looks him up and down.

"I'm not wearing that," she declares.

"Why?" Erik asks.

"Just look at it, for a start it. They could have just picked a plain black robe; they didn't have to add the blue and gold to it as well," Lizzie explains. A teacher walks over and hands them a robe each.

"You need to get ready; the ceremony starts in ten minutes," She informs them before walking off to hand some to another group. The boys all look at Lizzie, she notices.

"No, no way," she tells them.

"Why? I thought you said you wanted to experience everything. It's not a graduation if you don't wear the robe," Taylor says.

"I hate my life," Lizzie declares before walking off. She comes out a few minutes later, the boys all look at her in their robes.

"I think you look great," Erik tells her.

"Really?" She asks.

"Of course, you're the only person I know that could look good in anything," he responds.

"Just think about it this way. One hour in the robe and then we spend the night partying it up at prom," Taylor reminds her.

"But if we don't go now, we'll be late for our graduation," Jake informs them. They all start down the hall.

"Who's doing the speech?" Lizzie asks.

"They asked Mandy," Taylor answers.

"Of course, they did," Lizzie says.

At the graduation, Mandy is standing on stage reading her speech, Lizzie looks down the aisle at Taylor. He catches her eye and grins. When Mandy finishes, everyone gets ready to leave.

"So, Taylor who you going to prom with?" Lizzie asks.

"No one, I'm going alone," Taylor replies.

"Same, we should go alone together," Lizzie suggests. Taylor looks at her.

"That's a great idea," he responds.

Back at the Jones house, Alex and Vikki are in the living room, Sam comes downstairs in a suit.

"Where are you going?" Alex asks.

"Prom," Sam answers.

"But you don't go to the school anymore," Vikki reminds him.

"I know, but Evie asked me to go with her," Sam responds. Lizzie walks through the front door.

"Hey, look at you," she says to Sam.

"I know, I'm handsome. You don't need to tell me," Sam declares. Lizzie just shakes her head.

"Where are Hunter and Ben?" She asks.

"I'm not actually sure, they just sort of went out," Vikki tells her.

"Together?" Lizzie queries. Vikki nods.

"Okay, I'm going to get ready," Lizzie informs them.

"Wait, who you going with?" Alex asks.

"Taylor, but Jake and Erik will probably be with us too," Lizzie says heading upstairs. After a while, she comes down in her prom dress; the door goes, and Taylor walks in.

"Hey Lizzie, you don't mind if Erik and Jake come with us?" Taylor asks.

"Not at all," she answers heading towards the front door. Jake and Erik are standing outside with Evie.

"Sam, are you coming?" Lizzie asks. He gets up and leaves with them.

They arrive at the school and head into the hall.

"This actually looks amazing. As much as I dislike Mandy, she sure knows how to plan a party," Taylor says. Brooke runs over to them excitedly.

"Hey," she squeals.

"Hey, someone's excited," Jake responds.

"Who wouldn't be, this prom is amazing," Brooke tells them.

"I've seen better parties," Lizzie replies before walking away. As more people arrive the pace picks up, everyone starts dancing and chatting. After a while, the principal takes the stage.

"Can I have everyone's attention, in a minute I will be announcing your prom king and queen, but first I have a few words," he announces. Lizzie and Taylor are standing at the back of the hall.

"Bet you a tenner that Mandy is announced queen," Taylor whispers. Lizzie looks at him and he pulls a tenner out.

"You're on," she says. On the other side of the hall, Mandy is standing with Mia.

"Thank you for not running for prom queen this year," Mandy says to Mia.

"You're welcome, I know how bad you wanted this," Mia replies. The principal finishes his speech and pulls out two envelopes.

"And now the moment you've all been waiting for; this year proms queen is...Mia Pierce," he declares. Mandy looks at Mia who looks shocked.

"Mia, where are you?" The principal asks. Mia walks past Mandy and onto the stage. Lizzie looks at Taylor.

"Thank you," she says taking the money. Mandy looks across the hall at Lizzie. Lizzie smiles and waves.

"And your prom king is...Taylor Williamson," he announces, the hall cheers and Taylor goes on stage to accept his crown. After he's finished, he goes over to Lizzie.

"Was this you?" He asks pointing at the crown.

"No, it was all you," Lizzie replies. She notices Mandy and Mia leaving the hall.

"Give me a minute," she tells him before following them into the hallway.

"I can't believe you Mia, you know how much I wanted this," Mandy declares.

"Mandy, I don't know how I won, I didn't even start a campaign," Mia responds. Mandy glares at her.

"Well, you must have done something," she snaps. Lizzie comes around the corner.

"Sorry to interrupt, Mia your needed in the hall. It's time to dance with your prom king," she informs her, Mia heads off and Mandy looks at Lizzie.

"I should have known you were behind this," she states before storming off, Lizzie hears a hissing sound coming from the basement. She heads towards the basement door as she approaches it a hand touches her shoulder; she jumps and turns.

"Hunter!" She exclaims.

"Sorry I didn't mean to scare you. What are you doing?" He asks. Lizzie looks back towards the door.

"Nothing. Wait, what are you doing here?" She questions.

"I was just, looking for you," he tells her.

"Me? Why?" Lizzie queries.

"No reason, just wanted to check on you. Make sure you were having a good night," he answers. Lizzie studies him for a minute and then smiles.

"Uh-huh, in other words you were watching Taylor," she says.

"I have no idea what you're talking about," he responds. She steps towards him and leans towards his ear.

"You know exactly what I mean," she replies before walking off.

She enters the hall again and Sam walks over and holds his hand out.

"What?" Lizzie asks.

"I want to dance with my sister," Sam answers. Lizzie looks at him before taking his hand and heading to the dancefloor. He spins her around.

"What you did was nice," he informs her. She looks at him.

"I have no idea what you're talking about," she responds. Sam just smiles at her; an upbeat song comes on.

"I think you should ask your friend to dance," Sam tells her looks across the hall, she turns and sees Erik sitting alone. She approaches him, takes his hand and drags him on the dance floor. After a few hours of dancing and laughing, everyone heads home for the night.

The next morning, Lizzie heads downstairs, Alex, Vikki and Sam are standing next to the door.

"Are you leaving today?" She asks them.

"Yeah, are you sure you don't want to come?" Alex queries.

"I'm positive, I'm going to stay here with Hunter and Ben," she answers. He looks at her.

"I'll be fine, now go. Have fun, enjoy your summer. I'll be here when you get back," Lizzie demands pushing them out the door.

"Okay, okay. We're going," Alex says. They get in the car and drive off. Lizzie closes the door and turns around; Hunter and Ben are standing there.

"Are we alone?" Hunter asks, sitting on the sofa.

"Yes," Lizzie responds, joining him with Ben. They start chilling on the sofa when the doorbell rings.

"Are you expecting anyone?" Hunter asks.

"No," Lizzie answers, getting up. She goes over to the door and opens it.

"Hello Elizabeth," the man says at the door; she stares at him.

"Luke," she answers.